Robyn Schneider

better
than
yesterday

better
than
yesterday

Robyn Schneider

better than yesterday

Delacorte Press

Published by Delacorte Press
an imprint of Random House Children's Books
a division of Random House, Inc.
New York

Visit us on the Web! www.randomhouse.com/teens

Educators and librarians, for a variety of teaching tools, visit us at
www.randomhouse.com/teachers

The Library of Congress has cataloged the hardcover edition of this work as follows:
Schneider, Robyn.
Better than yesterday / Robyn Schneider. — 1st ed.
    p. cm.
Summary: Three seniors from an exclusive Connecticut prep school go to New York
City to find their runaway friend, and in the process discover themselves and the true
value of their friendship.
ISBN: 978-0-385-73345-8 (hardcover)
ISBN: 978-0-385-90362-2 (Gibraltar lib. bdg.)
[1. Coming of age—Fiction. 2. Self-actualization (Psychology)—Fiction.
3. Preparatory schools—Fiction. 4. Schools—Fiction. 5. Friendship—Fiction.
6. College choice—Fiction.] I. Title.
PZ7S36426Bet 2007
[Fic]—dc22   2006011654

ISBN: 978-0-385-73346-5 (tr. pbk.)

Printed in the United States of America

10 9 8 7 6 5 4 3 2 1

First Trade Paperback Edition

Mom, Dad,
this one's for you.

Hilliard School Song

We raise our song in praise of thee
Together this community
And we with bated breath await
Our failings, future, and our fate
And with respect to every rule
Due honor to fair Hilliard School.

And play we on the fields or courts
We cheer together all our sports
Always acting as sportsmen ought
Our games and matches fairly fought
With vict'ry laps by field or pool
We honor you, fair Hilliard School.

From hall to quad to chapel pew
The facets of our minds we hew
With classroom knowledge duly learned
And every grade honestly earned
With open hearts and logic cool
We sing your praises, Hilliard School.

Contents

• • • • • • • •

better
than
yesterday

1

Skylar: Out, Out, Damned Spotlight

Convocation was supposed to start at noon, and because the chapel didn't have air-conditioning and the gym was, well, a gym, the ceremony was set up on the grass out in Hamilton Quad with a makeshift stage and lots of white folding chairs.

But I wasn't sitting in the folding chairs with the rest of my classmates and their pastel-clad parents. I was on the stage, unfortunately trying to keep everyone in the front row from getting a free peep show of my panties (okay, thong), and wishing I'd worn a longer skirt. I was the senior honoree, which was supposedly a Very Big Deal because it meant I was ranked first in the incoming senior class and was getting tapped as the most likely candidate for valedictorian. Senior honoree was always a boy, and my presence on that stage, never mind the length of my skirt, was an unknown variable that many students were eagerly trying to solve.

Actually, the first-ranked boy in my class was Charley Morton, and I would rather have let him sit on the stage and take the award. I didn't want it. It was probably going to be a certificate. Hilliard Preparatory School couldn't have come up with something useful, like a gift card to Barnes & Noble? Or a Prada bag?

I glanced at the girl who was sitting on my left, this junior I'd never spoken to in my life, and said, "What do you think's the holdup? This ceremony is taking longer than a download of Janice Weiner's blog."

Random fact: Janice Weiner (presumably drunk at the time, though I shudder to guess her intentions if she had been sober) had posted half a dozen "lingerie model" pics of herself on her blog over spring break of our junior year. Someone saw them in her blog and sent the link as a mass e-mail to everyone with an @Hilliard.edu e-mail account. Such a scandal.

The girl I'd spoken to didn't say anything, so I sat there staring at my watch for the next three minutes until the first curl of music drifted through the quad. Some assholes, the same reckless upperclassmen who thought it was terrifically witty to hoot in assembly during the year, clapped and yelled in approval. The marching band, in their stiff white uniforms, traveled slowly forward as they blared the school song sans words.

As the band played, the door to Lerner Hall opened and the faculty who were staying on for summer session poured out in their ceremonial robes, caps, and hoods, which were probably still dirty from commencement two weeks ago. Mr. Bloom's robe definitely had a stain on the right shoulder. I wanted to give him a bar of soap and a squirt bottle of Febreze, then explain the difference.

Everyone's parents shifted in their seats so they could see

the colors on each teacher's hood and determine whether or not they approved of the degree, school, and major. Most of the students watched the faculty procession for a different reason: to see which teachers weren't doing summer session, and to see which teachers were new.

As if the information wasn't on the school Web site or in the crinkled programs on their laps.

As Headmaster Bell welcomed the "esteemed guests, distinguished faculty, and current Hilliard students" to the first day of summer session, I totally couldn't focus. It was so hot out, and everyone was staring at the stage, which meant that

> **Contention 1:** They were staring in my general direction, so
> **Subpoint A:** Chances were some of them were staring at me,
> **Subpoint B:** They could see up my skirt, and
> **Subpoint C:** They knew I was senior honoree.

Well, why shouldn't they know? I mean, I'd freaked when I found out about it, because I hadn't been trying to beat out Charley Morton or anything. It just happened. Like the whole eighties revival thing.

One day I was invisible, totally under the class rank radar and off everyone's secret hit lists of who they were going to blame next year if they didn't get into Princeton early decision. Then my mom got the letter in the mail. She almost didn't find it. We get a whole tub of mail a day, which the postman absolutely loves, because Mom is a literary agent and we're always getting manuscripts sent to the house. Tucked underneath a batch of query letters was an envelope with the Hilliard school crest.

Basically I was screwed. Everyone who put two and two together and got 4.0 today would realize that I had beat them out. Me. The girl who'd supposedly calculated the exact obtuse angle to which she spread her legs (more about that scandal later). Suddenly I would be their biggest threat. It was laughable, and what hurt me the most was that I couldn't deny the absurdity of the whole affair.

Finally Headmaster Bell ended his long-winded obey-the-rules-and-welcome-to-summer-session spiel and invited the quiet junior girl to sing the national anthem.

Polite clapping. She minced up to the lectern and planted her scuffed black flats with the toes against the wood, ruining them even more. Everyone stood up and placed their hand over their heart.

The same boys who had hooted earlier made whooping yells after she sang the words "land of the free," and I rolled my eyes. God. I was so ready for college.

After she finished with all those show-offy voice curls that the girls who never win on *American Idol* do, the girl sat down and an a cappella quartet led us in singing the school song, which I mouthed absently, a knot of nervousness in my stomach.

Bell took the lectern again. He had something in his hand. A certificate, big surprise. I tried to pay attention, but the heat was making my eyeliner smear, and my ass cheeks had formed covalent bonds with the chair. I wondered if my lack of focus meant I was going crazy, or if it was just too hot to concentrate.

> **Mental parliamentary debate number one:**
> Skylar Banks is going crazy—discuss.
> **Prime minister:** She cannot concentrate.
> Therefore, she is crazy.
> **Leader of the opposition:** She is stressed out and being stared at, so the lack of concentration is due to nerves.

"This student served as the copy editor of the *Hilliard Howler*. She is one of the senior class's sixty-five National Merit Scholars and last year's Policy Debate state semifinalist. This year's senior honoree, from Tarrytown, New York, Skylar Banks."

I stood up, gave my skirt a good yank into place, then tottered over to the lectern on my mint green Miu Miu espadrilles and shook Bell's hand.

People clapped, but that still didn't drown out the sounds of half the student body whispering furiously—about me. I caught a glimpse of my parents in the front near Alison Forsyth, my sworn enemy. I privately thought she was the highlight of the ceremony, because I'd heard her complain earlier, "Omigod, I'm so bored I could shoot myself in the head with a knife."

Mom was wearing her New York literary agent uniform: a pantsuit and pearls. Dad looked even more uncomfortable.

Ever the Sarah Lawrence German professor, he wore a linen jacket and crocheted flat-bottomed tie.

My parents and I are obviously not related. I mean, my fashion sense clashes with their careers. Actually, so does my math gene.

I walked back to my seat and ran my fingers over the raised school seal on the certificate, wondering who had penned my name on that line in such elegant calligraphy, and if they wondered why it was my name they were writing. Above my head, a banner with the school gonfalon on it floated languidly. Carefully, without chipping my French manicure, I traced the same design on my certificate until convocation ended.

Afterward, there was this reception by the lake, under the white canopy Hilliard usually reserved for alumni who came out to the Hilliard-Hotchkiss regatta in their old school ties and then insisted on giving their families a tour of the dormitory. I stood under the canopy and watched the other students wander around with their parents, who were eating pastries from the dessert and coffee tables.

Random fact: the ladies in the caf lace the brownies with laxatives. Swear to God. At the end of any school function, there were always twice as many brownies left on the trays as other desserts, because everyone was afraid to touch them.

Mom was off talking with Mrs. Buchanan, one of the English teachers, whose (and I quote) "greatest joy in life is the proper punctuation of perfect prose." Dad was staying close to me, drinking black coffee from a Styrofoam cup. He kept talking about his new translation of *The Sorrows of Young Werther* while I clutched my certificate and looked around to see who had come to summer session.

A lot of the teachers were there, sans robes (not like the faculty blazers were much better). Headmaster Bell was smiling at some alumni fathers with their terrified-looking freshman sons and had his hand on the shoulder of a guy who looked like a J. Crew model. Hmmm. I hoped Mr. Seersucker Button-Down was the new creative-writing teacher.

I glanced around some more, trying to find my roommate. Rising seniors were the smallest turnout. Everyone was probably off on those missions to third-world countries, trying to get an edge over the competition for a spot at Yale, or whatever else their private admissions counselors had told them to do.

It was strange, but while I was standing there listening to my dad happily lecture me, I felt like there was someone behind me. Someone I knew. I turned around.

Blake Dorsey, whom I hadn't seen since freshman year, was leaning against one of the tables. He looked stoned and tan, very West Coast.

"The reader assumes the role of Wilhelm, creating a duality—"

"Dad, I see a friend of mine," I said, interrupting. "Be back in a few minutes."

I walked over to Blake and watched him smile as he saw me. "Skylar!"

We hugged, and he squeezed me tightly. When we pulled apart, I stared at him. He had the same soft brown curls, but he was taller, thinner, his jaw lean and his chin almost covered by a goatee, an older version of the boy I used to know well. The collar on his Lacoste shirt was popped in that annoying über-preppy way, and he wore khaki Abercrombie shorts with deck shoes.

A little about Blake: He used to go to Hilliard as a freshman, but I hadn't heard from him since then. When he left, no one knew what had happened, where he went, or if he was coming back.

We were pretty good friends as freshmen because he was cute and I thought that mattered back then, even though I wasn't interested in dating him. He also liked to pull pranks— we were co-conspirators. Our best was probably when we wedged a blow-up doll through the space between the locked glass doors of the trophy case and then inflated it with a bicycle pump.

Blake's family was from Corona Del Mar, California, and had a lot of money, the sheer volume of which made it okay to openly discuss. Blake always used to be paranoid he'd misplace the Visa card he had on his dad's account and someone would buy a fleet of BMWs before the limit kicked in. His dad used to own some company that had to do with wireless technology. Rumor was that Microsoft had bought it.

Blake also had an older brother, Kyle, who'd been a senior when we were freshmen. Kyle had been lacrosse captain and got into Yale early. Also, he'd kind of been my boyfriend, and was the catalyst for my reputation as a slut. A reputation, and reason, Blake had no idea about. I didn't want him to think I'd betrayed our friendship, snuck around behind his back, and lied to him. And I intended to keep it that way.

"I can't believe you're back," I said. "What are you doing here?"

"I'm teaching here now. Y'know, I was such a genius I finished high school and college in two years, and now I'm back to teach sex ed."

"Oh, *that* must be why your ceremonial hood was the color of bullshit. Seriously, though. Why?"

"The guidance counselor at my other school was a total dick, and the only reason my brother got into Yale was because of the letter of rec he got from Mr. Harcourt, so Mom decided I had to come back here."

That couldn't be it. Everyone knew the only thing Mr. Harcourt was good at was consoling parents whose kids got waitlisted or deferred.

I frowned and asked, "So what are you taking at summer session?"

"Philosophy and Moral Issues, for the religion requirement. And the creative-writing class with the new teacher."

"I have creative writing with Mr. McCabe, too. I think Charley and Marissa might be in our class," I said, tossing out the names of our respective roommates from freshman year.

Blake's eyes opened a millimeter wider, like he actually thought we were all still hanging out together and having study sessions with vending-machine Chex Mix and a tub of skinny highlighters. Yeah, as though everything was just the way he'd left it, and we were waiting for him to come back and take his role as Blake Dorsey, our fearless leader. Please.

"You guys are still tight?" Blake asked, and I tried not to roll my eyes.

"Not really. God. Marissa's still around, but Charley not so much. We're on the debate team together, though. Everything's over, Blake. Things fall apart."

"Sure." Blake looked disoriented. Then his eyes focused and he nodded at my chest. "What's that?"

I looked down, wondering if bird poop had dropped onto my boobs and I was walking around looking like a park bench or something.

The certificate. I'd forgotten about it.

"Oh, I'm senior honoree. Weren't you there?"

"Nah, I got here just in time for the free Ex-Lax brownies."

But I wasn't so sure. I averted my gaze, remembering. Convocation. Blake had shown up late, but he'd been there. He'd been in the back and hadn't taken a seat.

"Yeah, whatever. You were totally at convocation."

"Are you sure you don't have eyes in the back of your head?" Blake joked.

I shrugged.

"Well, Miss Supersight, it sure is good to be back at Mutant High," Blake teased, easily slipping into the banter from freshman year.

I shivered slightly, even though it was warm out. His brother used to make that joke, used to call me the Mutant because I was the only freshman in honors pre-calc. It was creepy, hearing Blake say it so nonchalantly, unaware of what I'd done with his brother.

"Are you cold?" Blake asked. Then he lowered his eyes and hooted, "You are."

"Oh my God. You horndog!" I folded my arms across my chest, which was awkward because I still had the certificate. Blake stared at the certificate.

"Charley must be freaking out now, huh? That kid was going to be senior honoree for sure, I thought."

"Me too."

"Yeah, but you were always smarter than everyone gave you credit for."

He smirked, as though he thought I was going to swoon and throw myself at him, cold boobs and all, just because of one lousy compliment.

"Listen," Blake said, "I've got to get some shit out of my car. See you later?"

"Okay. Later."

I watched him walk away toward the parking lot, probably to go smoke a bowl or listen to his emo California-boy music. I wondered where his parents were, why they hadn't come, and the real reason for Blake's return. But the reception was slowing to a trickle of activity, and it was time to find my parents and move into my dorm for the next six weeks. Time for everything to begin.

2

Charley: For Those About to Rock the Boat, We Salute You

My mom almost didn't let me bring my guitar to summer session because of the SAT. For most of my life, I'd had a theory that you multiply your IQ times ten and that's what you score on the SAT. And my Standford-Binet score was 160. So there you go.

Then some idiot decided to mess with the SAT and ruin my theory and generally destroy my life when he changed the test to be out of 2400. Of course my parents expected me to get the 2400. They also expected me to be senior honoree and do Harvard pre-med.

I got my score the first weekend of summer, two days before summer session started. I was home in Massachusetts. My mother got back early from her practice (she's a psychologist), baked some crap she called blond brownies, and assembled the whole family to watch me check my score online.

So there I was, sitting at the kitchen table with my laptop, trying to find the one inch of Wi-Fi reception in the house, with Mom, Dad, and my kid brother, Ben, breathing down my neck.

I typed in the College Board's URL, entered my user name and alphanumeric password, and waited for the results.

During those five seconds it took the page to load, I could literally feel all the pressure my family had heaped on my shoulders over the last three years to get a 5 on every AP test, to star in all the school plays, to qual for nationals in International Extemporaneous Debate, to be senior honoree and then valedictorian, and to get a perfect score on my SAT.

Dad had his hand on my shoulder, and he was gripping me like I was on the brink of losing his law firm a major client, my T-shirt pulled tight around my neck and balled up in his fist. The screen loaded. I'd scored an 800 on verbal—good. Another 800 on the writing. I'd done it! I scrolled down. My math section was a 730. Holy shit.

Dad stopped gripping my shirt. Mom gasped. Ben kept cracking his knuckles like the little creep he was.

"I thought you prepared for this, Charley," Dad said.

"I did prepare. I just screwed up."

"How can you 'just screw up'?" Dad demanded. "You practice enough, the knowledge becomes rote, and you succeed. It's exactly the same as debate or drama."

"I'm sorry," I said.

"Sorry? Think of the future, Charley. You can't apologize for malpractice. Do you expect to say sorry if you make a mistake in the OR, or if you misdiagnose a patient?" Dad pressed.

"I guess not. I'll try harder. I understand how important it is to get everything exactly right."

Mom, who had been silent the whole time, took a deep breath and said, "It'll be fine. Pack your SAT prep books for summer session, huh, sweetie? If you take a math practice test every day for the rest of the summer, you'll get that twenty-four hundred."

"Uh-huh. Sure."

Suddenly I was drained. I didn't want to have this conversation anymore. Yeah, I'd messed up, but I didn't need to be simultaneously cross-examined and psychoanalyzed. I stared at Mom, silently appealing to her to make Dad get off my case. I thought it had worked when Mom stood up, but then she said, "Well, I guess we won't be needing these, then."

Mom threw away those gross blond brownies and wandered into the den with Dad and Ben. I stared at that screen until my login expired. How had it happened? How had I choked on the math section?

After the computer told me to log in again, I switched it off and went to my bedroom. I pulled my black Fender electric guitar out from my still-packed school trunk, slammed the volume up on my amp, and just whaled on the thing.

The second my fingertips pressed down on the metal strings I felt better. There was no pressure to play the guitar. I didn't have to be straight-A at that. I started a complicated riff and contorted my face like a rock star. *Take that, David Bowie!*

"Can you turn that down and start studying for your retest?" Mom yelled through the door.

I felt this anger build up inside me, like the time Dad had told me I had to take French and Latin at the same time to be competitive for Harvard. Harvard! Since I'm from Somerville, I've lived in the shadow of Harvard and MIT for most of my life. It's not exciting, it's not different, and it's not rock and roll.

I wasn't going to stop playing, not even if I wound up as salutatorian or got deferred from early decision to the regular applicant pool. So I took off my sweaty T-shirt, rolled it up, stuffed it in the crack under the door, turned off my amp, and kept playing my guitar. My parents never knew I wasn't studying.

But when I walked out to the car two days later with my guitar case slung over my shoulder and carrying my amp and distortion pedal, ready for the drive to Hilliard, Mom practically shat a whole pan of blond brownies.

"Absolutely not, Charley! Why did your father and I ever buy you that horrible thing? You'll be playing it when you should be studying."

"We're not sending you off to summer camp," Dad added.

"Mom, come on. I need to practice. And I'll only play on weekends."

"I'm sorry, Charley. You need to be serious about college."

"I'm serious. I'm fucking serious, I swear. Dad, tell her I'm serious."

My dad stopped punching buttons on our SUV's GPS only long enough to warn me to watch my language.

"Okay. Fine. I won't take my guitar. But then I won't be able to compete in Parli next year as a secondary event."

"What?" Dad asked.

Mom looked upset. My bullshit had better work.

"Pete Donahue, who ranked top five in state last year for Parliamentary Debate? His partner graduated. I told Pete I'd bring my guitar to summer session, since he plays bass, and we could practice together. If he thinks I'm not dependable, he'll partner with Skylar Banks or someone else."

"Fine. Get in the car, Charley. We don't want to be late to convocation," Dad said.

I smiled and climbed in the back with my guitar. Yeah, my parents ran my life, but I could get away with a few things. Pete Donahue had quit Parli and switched his main event to Lincoln-Douglas Debate after his partner graduated. I doubted he played a harmonica, much less a bass.

After the convocation debacle, I told my parents that I wanted to move into my dorm before my roommate (person unknown) did, so I could have some quiet time to study, and they believed me. Mom, Dad, and Ben (Hilliard-bound eighth grader, and soon to be my replacement in dear M&D's vicarious life) helped me lug my stuff into Milbank Hall 37 instead of going to the reception. We were barely talking to each other after the ceremony.

God, it wasn't my fault that Skylar Banks beat me out for senior honoree. That girl took honors pre-calc as a freshman, giving her GPA an unfair edge that no one else had. It wasn't like I'd failed. I had the highest GPA of any boy in my class. But they didn't see it that way. All they saw was a girl with high heels and a too-short skirt accepting an award that should have gone to their son. Me.

Even worse was that I got this perverse thrill out of seeing Skylar up there. Not because I wanted my parents to kill me, or because I'm a pervert, but because she was so goddamn cute.

She looked shy and embarrassed, like she didn't want to be up there. *And* she looked hot. Skylar was the sultry New York sex goddess of the senior class. And not because of getting caught with the lax captain her freshman year, or that rumor about her and the rest of the lacrosse team, which was a load of crap. The thing with Skylar was that she was effortless. She didn't mean to get straight A's, or to place at all the debate tournaments, or to look so amazing, or to make me fall in love with her.

I shouldn't even have been *thinking* about her. Skylar was the reason my parents didn't think I was good enough. She was the one thing standing in my way, preventing me from being the valedictorian. And I had hardly talked to her for the past two years. I was a wreck, an absolute mess.

I stared at my suitcase and duffel bag, thinking how good it was to be back at Hilliard. Some guys on the debate team called it Helliard, but they were wrong. Hilliard was paradise, because it meant that my parents were in a different state and that as long as I did everything they asked, I could have the leftover margins of my A-plus papers to do my own thing. Like obsess over Skylar. Or rock on my guitar.

I unzipped the duffel bag of school-approved attire, which my mom had packed. In a fit of anal-retentiveness, she had placed my polo shirts in plastic bags by color: two navy blue, two dark green, two white. The slippery supersized Ziploc bags were ridiculous. It looked like my mom had freeze-dried, then shrink-wrapped every piece of my uniform.

Next I tackled my suitcase, which I'd packed myself. Sheet music tumbled out of the zipper pockets. I took out my iPod, iPod speakers, Harvard sweatshirt (I know, but it was the most comfortable thing I owned), flannel pajamas, jeans, new sneakers, graphing calculator, pencils, big red *Ten Real SATs* book, and big white *Official Study Guide for the New SAT.*

Yeah, I'm the kind of nerd who preps for SAT prep. Don't judge; I'll take you down using my debate trophies like nunchucks. Just because I'm a six-foot, blond, bespectacled, skinny white boy doesn't mean I can't render you concussed with my first-place International Extemporaneous varsity state quals trophy.

I reached for my guitar, even though I knew I should be timing my test-taking prowess before my roommate showed up and started banging around and unpacking.

As I unhooked the hard leather case and lifted ol' Black and White out, I instantly felt calm. The smooth metal strings slid easily under my callused fingertips as I played carelessly, without a pick or an amp. I swear to God, the music was so muted and perfect it felt like the first moment I'd found out that video games had secret codes (up, up, down, down, left, right, left, right, B, A, start, I still remember). I played an old Weezer song with my eyes closed, fingers flying over the fretboard with no mistakes.

The mattress springs groaned slightly as I finished the song and laid the guitar across the blanket I'd been sitting on. Sighing and hating myself for it, I sat down at my desk, turned on my graphing calculator, and tackled the first problem in the *Ten Real SATs* practice test number 2.

Half an hour later, when I was just about to finish the first math section, the doorknob rattled and someone said, "Whassup, Masshole?"

Blake Dorsey kicked the door open and stood there like Banquo's ghost, scaring the living shit out of me. I'd never expected to see my frosh roommate again, especially not two years later.

Blake was wearing a duffel bag slung across each shoulder, making him look like he had strapped on a bunch of army ammo.

"Shit, man, I didn't know you were back," I said, smiling even though this really wussy voice in the back of my head was cursing because Blake had interrupted my practice test and basically rendered it worthless.

"Now ya know. Good to be back. I knew things didn't fall apart, since we're rooming together again."

"What are you talking about?" I asked as I watched him kick his still-packed bags into his closet.

"Nothing. Something Skylar said." He didn't bother to shut the closet.

As I stood there like Magically Immobile Man, Blake picked up my guitar and sat down on his naked mattress. (What a screwed-up word association, huh? *Naked* and *mattress*. *Naked* and *mattress* and *Skylar Banks*. No. Shut up, brain.) He bent over the guitar and plucked at it halfheartedly. (Now this is just a really gross musing. We've got *naked* and *mattress* and *Skylar* and *Blake* and *plucking*. Ugh.)

"You're a regular Hendrix," I said sarcastically, wincing as I heard my high E string go out of tune from Blake's fumbling fingers.

"I know, right? I'm opening for Death Cab next week."

Blake dropped the guitar on his bed and opened a window. He fumbled in his pockets and came out with a pack of Parliaments and a cheap red lighter.

"No, come on," I said, knowing I sounded lame. "Not in the room."

But I knew the drill. He used to do this all the time when we were freshmen.

"Got it covered, dude," Blake said, nodding at the open window. He held the cigarette as though it were a joint and sucked hard on the inhale. Then he passed me the cigarette.

As a card-carrying member of the Hilliard debate team, drama club, and newspaper staff, I wasn't exactly a seasoned smoker. Still, it was Blake's way of bonding. He'd never noticed freshman year that I didn't inhale, so I figured the trick would still work. I took a small bit of smoke into my mouth, felt my eyes water, and passed the cigarette back.

We stood side by side at the window, and it felt strange to have a roommate again. I'd had a single room since sophomore year, but had signed up late for summer session and been assigned a double. Blake and I had managed pretty well when we lived together as freshmen, though, so I figured this wasn't exactly a Harvard-rejection-letter-caliber catastrophe.

"Hey, did you see Skylar onstage today?" I asked, hoping I didn't come across as a bitter jerk about her being senior honoree.

"Convocation? Yeah. Pretty sexy."

"Yeah, we haven't had a senior honoree that hot since Jonas Winegardener," I joked, but then I realized that I had agreed with Blake about Skylar being cute. No, not cute. Hot. Shit.

"Winegardener? Didn't he wear headgear?"

"Yeah." I laughed. "Like I said, nothing hotter than metal wrapped around your head in this damn heat."

Blake smiled.

"So about Skylar," Blake said, "did you and her ever get it on?"

Even though the question was asked nonchalantly, I knew he wanted my answer to be no.

"No." But I wished. And apparently so did Blake.

"Sucks," he said, but he didn't seem like he thought it sucked at all. "From the looks of you, you could've used a little real-life porn fest, Charley boy."

"What? I'm a hundred percent sex god. Check out these transition lenses," I quipped.

But yeah. He had a point.

"So what've you been up to, anyway?"

"Debate team, the school plays, drama club, honor society, the *Howler*. You know, typical Hilliard stuff. What about you?"

"Oh, partying, getting laid, drunk, high, what have you. Hanging out with friends back in Cali. Lots of crazy times."

Blake was quiet for a moment. I could sense him thinking, and for the first time, I actually wondered how much Blake had changed from the sarcastic rich-boy prankster he'd been as a freshman.

"So, Charley," Blake said, "when was the last time you just hung out? Y'know, did normal stuff with people? And I don't mean studying."

I kept quiet and waited. It was like in Policy Debate: shut up and let your opposition skewer himself.

"Why don't we invite Skylar and Marissa over to watch a DVD tonight? How about it? We can chill."

That actually wasn't a bad idea.

"Sure. We can ask them at dinner."

"Fantabulous."

Blake lit another cigarette and flopped onto his mattress, staring at the ceiling and blowing smoke rings quietly. Holden Caulfield meets Gandalf the Grey.

Grabbing my SAT prep stuff, I left Blake to contemplate his own crap, and headed down to the boathouse.

3

Skylar: Of Mice and Mensa Members

My espadrilles were giving me blisters from hell. So it was a good thing that Dad carried most of my stuff into the dorm.

I had Milbank Hall 21, which was the big corner room. Milbank, the main dorm, was co-ed by floor, and some asshole boy who lived below me kept banging something against his ceiling (aka my floor) to say hello. Charming.

Dad dumped a suitcase on one of the beds as I stuck my head out the window and yelled, "Milbank eleven, you suck!"

A boy who looked like a freshman and his chubby roommate poked their heads out the window and looked up at me, laughing.

Ugh. Fourteen-year-olds.

"Whatever, losers. Keep it in your pants or I'll jump up and down at three in the morning."

"Skylar," my dad warned.

"Don't be vulgar," Mom added.

God. I couldn't say anything around them.

"Hi," someone said softly from the doorway.

I leaned back into the room and saw my roommate for the summer, Marissa Rodolf (aka Fantasy Freako, but in a nice way), kicking a gigantic duffel bag with crisp airline tags through the doorway.

A little about Marissa: Marissa spent her breaks with her three younger siblings and parents in Portland, Oregon. Her mom and dad ran some computer business out of their house and taught computer science at a community college. Marissa was on scholarship.

Justification of previous statement: Not like I was judging or anything. It didn't really matter what tax bracket someone's parents were in, so long as they were smart in class and not all bitchy toward people who did come from money. Or at least that was how I felt about it.

There were the scholarship kids, some of whom were totally bitter about money, talked about it all the time, and grouped together; then there were the middle-of-the-road kids, who pretended they had all this money and worked summers in retail to buy last season's Marc Jacobs at an employee discount; and then there were the super-rich, whose parents owned things that everyone had heard of. My parents each made a decent salary and we had a nice house in Westchester, which excluded me from basically every wealth-based social category at Hilliard. I was stuck halfway between the middle-of-the-roaders and the super-rich.

Of course, the class divisions weren't totally rigid. Like, debate team was debate team, and crew was crew. And, after a few semesters at Hilliard, no one asked what your parents did anymore. By then, enough time had passed that we existed on our own reputations, rather than our parents' bank statements. And my reputation was currently more scandalous than the latest celebrity gossip: slut who stole the senior honoree title and roomed with geek-girl Marissa.

Marissa, on the other hand, was a total virgin who didn't think that boys, like, masturbated. Ever. Marissa was addicted to all those fantasy books like the Chronicles of Narnia and Artemis Fowl and especially Harry Potter. Her fan fiction and poetry spilled out of her journals and onto Web sites like GreatestJournal and DeviantArt and FictionPress. Her screen name was JedixDragonxPrincess.

Marissa and I had been roommates freshman year, and I liked to read as much as she did (we swapped back then), but I got smart about it. If you wanted to read without everyone making fun of you for being a huge nerd, you had to read classics. That way it looked like an assignment. Kerouac, Vonnegut, Kafka—those were all fine. You could pass for studious with those. But *Dealing with Dragons*? Everyone knew right away that you were an antisocial little book freak co-existing in a world where every mermaid had perfect tits and all the little witches and wizards stayed virgins until they were married.

Even so, I totally got along with Marissa because compared to her everyone was morally corrupt. She didn't care about my reputation. She was a nice girl who seemed to genuinely like me. And I was dying to attack her French braid and pluck her eyebrows. Maybe while she slept?

"Hi," I said, trying not to sigh as I took in her outfit: Birkenstocks, khaki knee-length skirt, striped rugby shirt.

"Nice to see you again, Marissa," my dad said, winking as he lifted a stack of deliciously thick books onto my shelf.

"Hi, Professor Banks, Mrs. Banks. How was the drive?"

Marissa chatted with my parents about their jobs as she unpacked and stuck a *Lord of the Rings* poster with a map of Middle Earth over her bed.

"It's not straight," I told her. "The left side needs to go down."

By the time we got the poster straight, my parents were ready to leave. They looked sad, as if I wasn't coming home in just six weeks. Or maybe that wasn't the reason. My parents had never pushed me when they found out my IQ, but even without rushing off to college early, my high school years were drawing to a close. This was it, the first of many lasts, the beginning of the end.

I hugged them goodbye. My dad was all, *"Auf Wiedersehen."* I swear, Dad was the reason I took Spanish for my language requirement.

"You aren't usually at summer session," I said to Marissa, busily hanging my *Sex and the City* poster over my bed.

"Yeah, because the best cons are in the summer."

I stared at her like, *Huh?* Convicts? Converse? Contraception?

"Sorry, conventions. Fantasy and sci-fi stuff. But this year we've got that new creative-writing class, so I thought I'd come."

"You know who's taking creative writing?" I asked, watching her place a stuffed green dragon on top of her homemade quilt.

"You?"

"Well, besides me."

"Who?"

"Blake Dorsey."

"What? He came back? You're kidding!"

"Nope. I saw him at the reception. Swear to God."

"Was it love at first sight? Did he spot you across the crowded buffet tables and sweep you off your feet?" She giggled and rolled her eyes at her own dramatics.

"Ugh, not even. Marissa, you are such a nerd! Have you been reading those teen romances again?"

"I'm just saying. He liked you when we were freshmen."

"No he didn't. We were friends. I could never date him."

Um, yeah. I couldn't date him because I'd lost my OV (oral virginity) with his brother.

"Okayyyyyy."

"Mariss!"

"I was just checking. It would be weird if you two started going out. I mean, he doesn't know about you and Kyle, right?"

"Of course not." Thank God.

"That's good. But anyway, he was so in love with you back in ninth grade. I bet he still is."

"You think everyone likes me. Remember when you said Pete Donahue had a crush on me because he sat next to me on the car ride to state quals? Or Ali Ahmad, because he asked me to join the chess league? Or Charley Morton? Puh-leeze."

"Everyone *does* like you, Skylar."

"Why?" I asked, genuinely curious.

Marissa turned Barbie Dream House pink.

"Tell me!" I insisted.

"Well—" She put her face in her hands. "Well, first of all, you have big boobs."

"Oh my God. I cannot believe you just said that. I do not have big boobs." They weren't enormous, but my boobs were kind of, um, prominent.

Marissa gave me a look like, *Oh really?* Then she burst out laughing. Honestly, it wasn't *that* funny.

"Okay," I said, grabbing my Longchamp tote. "I'm going down to the lake while you have a laughing fit over the size of my Victoria's Secret demi. See you at dinner."

I'd discovered the back of the old boathouse at the end of September of my freshman year, when I was crying over a B-plus on my first English paper and didn't want anyone to see me. My parents wouldn't care about the B, but I did. I'd been so sure of myself and of the five-paragraph essay structure my eighth-grade English teacher had drilled into me. After that, I learned to over-research, use the full page for my works cited, analyze more than comment, and always come up with an original paper topic. My two-page papers turned into five-page theses, and my B-pluses turned into A-pluses, which I savored quietly in class.

Some crew alumni had donated money for a new boathouse back in the late nineties, so the old one had been abandoned. I liked to sit there and study, or read fashion magazines or the embarrassing academic books I checked out of the school library and didn't want anyone to know I was reading for fun, flipping pages too fast to be normal. Back then I'd wanted to be normal and fit in so badly that I felt it like a dull ache in my chest every time I didn't raise my hand to answer a question. I'd thought normal was cool, like highlights or a St. Barts tan.

This time, I sat with my back against the peeling clapboards of the boathouse and watched the white tent being taken down across the lake, where the reception had been. I was sitting on my tote bag, because I'd stupidly forgotten to grab a towel, and I was kind of smoking a clove.

I liked the taste of the sugar on my lips, the feel of the brown paper between my fingers, like a sharpened number-two pencil poised over a math test. I didn't really inhale, except to light the thing. It was comforting to hold on to something that made me feel worse and better at the same time.

After a little while of sitting there and reflecting more than my compact mirror, I heard someone mutter, "Crap!"

Whoa. I'd thought I was by myself. I got up, still holding the clove, and wandered around to the other side of the boathouse.

"Charley?"

Charley Morton was sprawled over an SAT prep book with a red marker in his hand. His glasses were slipping down his nose and his hair was tousled and sticking up all over the place.

"Hey."

He snapped the book shut, as though he didn't want me to see how many questions he'd missed (my guess: one).

"You know, I could make a joke about how you're a prep

doing SAT prep at a prep school, but then I'd sound like an idiot," I said, fake-inhaling on my clove.

Charley smiled and said, "Congratulations on senior honoree. Really. I bet your parents are proud." He sounded sincere yet sad, the way he always did when I placed first in a debate tournament, even though we didn't compete in the same event.

"You mean Herr Dad and Agent Mom? They could care less," I said, tugging on my skirt, which was riding up my hipbones. "They're happy and all, but they weren't expecting it. It's like everything I do surprises them."

Things that surprise my parents:
- My talent for math, rather than literature
- Winning senior honoree
- That I can walk in stilettos
- That I know the difference between Gucci and Pucci
- My insistence on attending MIT next year
- That I would rather read *Vogue* than Goethe, but only when no one wants to discuss George Canter's set theory
- My SAT score (a perfect 2400)
- The fact that I've never exactly had a "real boyfriend" but am kind of experienced (not like they know this, but if they did, it would totally surprise them)

I let them convince me to take creative writing during summer session just to shut Mom up about what a "wonderful surprise" my SAT score was.

I snapped out of my mental list as Charley said, "Seriously, though. Congrats on senior honoree."

It was so tragic! The poor guy was killing himself to be nice, so I said, "Thanks, but it should have been you. I didn't deserve it."

"No, you did. You're smart."

"I'm not smart; I'm a Polaroid," I self-deprecated in the way you're supposed to at Hilliard.

Charley laughed and ran a hand through his hair.

"You won't guess who my roommate is," he told me.

Why not be ridiculous?

"Must be Blake Dorsey," I joked, but as soon as I said it, I realized it was true.

"How did you know?"

"Today's totally back-asswards. Like, the whole senior honoree thing. Plus we're both living with our freshman-year roomies."

"This is true," Charley said seriously, staring over his shoulder at the lake.

I brought the clove to my lips again.

"You shouldn't smoke," he told me.

"I don't inhale. It's just something to do. Makes me feel like a character out of a film noir."

"Wouldn't you rather be a character from some current teen TV drama and quit smoking those things?"

I sighed and tossed the butt on the ground.

"Charley," I pleaded, "put it out for me?"

"Are you kidding?"

"Do you know how expensive these shoes were?"

He winked and crushed the cigarette under his sandal, and for a second I thought he was cuter than I gave him credit for being, but then I remembered how I was a slut who had bad luck with boys. So never mind. I couldn't inflict any more pressure on poor Charley.

We chatted a little about the new SAT, and I didn't mention my scores because I thought it would stress him out even more. After a half hour of just talking back and forth, I wondered why I didn't consider Charley one of my close friends anymore. When had he changed from the type of friend whose door I would knock on before heading to the dining hall to the type of friend I said hi to in the hallways and didn't always stop to chat with?

Probably around the time I switched from maxi-pads to tampons.

Random fact: When I was really little, I used to call Tampa, Florida, where my mom's parents lived, "Tampon, Florida," because that's what it sounded like when Mom said it. Mom encouraged this, saying I was creative and using metaphors to express myself.

After a while Charley glanced at his watch, mouthed three, two, one, and then cocked his head as the bells chimed, signaling ten minutes until dinner. I looked down at the leaves that were clinging to my outfit like I'd been having a tumble in a pile of foliage, but suddenly I didn't care. Everything was wrecked after having to sit onstage, anyway. After everyone had moved on from my drama to Janice Weiner's last year, I'd thought I could rebuild. Be social again, and maybe even trust myself to have a real boyfriend, although I didn't have anyone in mind. But now everyone at summer session knew my name and knew what I was: a nerd. An anal, overly studious nerd hiding behind designer footwear and eyeliner, who was going to take their spot at [insert Ivy League school here].

We walked together toward the dining hall, which was sandwiched between the chapel and gymnasium, forming a circle of large, elegant stone buildings with thick, ancient windows. As we were walking through Hamilton Quad, Charley's pocket vibrated.

He flipped a sleek silver phone open and said, "What up?"

After a few seconds, Charley said, "Not yet, but I will. Hey, Skylar and I are just about at Brooks Quad. Wait a sec, okay?"

I raised a perfectly plucked eyebrow at him and asked, "Well?"

"Come on, let's catch up with Blake."

We walked a little faster, and I became sure of one thing: espadrilles are the most sadistic form of torture except maybe that thing where sorority pledges have to stand in bathing suits and let frat boys circle all the fatty parts of their bodies in permanent marker. Or converting linear functions to point-slope form.

"Does Blake seem different to you?" I asked Charley, remembering how he'd avoided explaining where he'd been and why he'd come back, when the old Blake had loved to talk about himself.

"Yeah. Darker, maybe. But we're all growing up, right?"

"Tell that to Marissa."

"True."

We made a left past Lerner Hall and came out in Brooks Quad, where Blake was leaning against a tree with one leg up in an affected-yet-casual way. The dining hall was at the far end of Brooks. Students in khakis or skirts and collared shirts (what is it with popped collars? They seriously make you look like a vicar or Dracula, neither of which was popular this season) lounged around, taking photos of each other on their camera phones, hugging each other hello and chatting.

A bunch of people stared at me, and some yelled congratulations, which embarrassed me. Worse were the students who deliberately turned away when I walked by, or who fell silent when I passed them. I kept hearing snatches of muttered conversations that I was sure had to do with me. I stared at the ground, and tried to look humble and uncomfortable (not like it involved much acting). It was fine to dress crazy or listen to showtunes or draw manga, but to stick out by being "better" than everyone else was unforgivable. To be cocky about it was even worse, and to be a cocky girl, doubly so.

"Do you ever wonder what it was like when this place was single-sex?" I asked, and Blake's laughter echoed through the room.

"A regular sausage fest."

"Yeah, okay." I rolled my eyes as we took seats at a long rectangular table against one of the walls.

Marissa wandered over a few minutes later and sat down with us.

"Hi, Blake," she said. "Haven't seen you for a while."

"Really?" Blake joked, forking a lump of macaroni and cheese onto his plate and passing the family-style bowl to Charley. "Because I seem to remember a certain ménage à trois this afternoon in your room."

"Huh?" Marissa asked, frowning.

I sighed. Was it always my job to rescue her from the seedy underworld that is the mind of teenage boys?

"Nothing. Blake's playing a character again. Excuse him."

"Excuse yourself," Blake retorted, and my laughter exploded into my water glass, because it was exactly the sort of thing he used to say when we were freshmen.

"Excuse your mother," I joked back.

"Why don't we get off mothers? I just got off yours," Charley followed up.

We stared at Marissa, waiting.

"That's because, um, because your mother's like Excalibur—everyone wants a turn trying to, um, loosen her up."

"Oh my God," I said, because that was one weird-as-hell joke. "Marissa!"

"What?"

"Where did you learn that?"

"An online RPG."

"That's cool," Charley said, winking at me to show he was okay with my roomie being an über-dork, as opposed to a regular nerd. "RPGs are like acting."

"That's right," I said, spearing a salad leaf with my dull fork. "Blake, you missed Charley in all the plays. He totally rocked in *The Foreigner*. And he was in *Once upon a Mattress* as—what was it?—Prince Dauntless. Very Broadway."

"Thanks," Charley said, blushing. Awww, he was doing that cuter-than-I-want-him-to-be thing again.

"And the last one he did? *Rumors?* Amazing."

"Yeah, but did you see the program?" Charley asked. "They put me down as 'Charles Morton the Third.' I sounded like a pretentious ass. And I still can't get the school to put 'Charley Morton' on my schedule."

"Speaking of schedules, does everyone have McCabe at nine a.m. tomorrow?" Blake asked.

We all nodded.

"Helliard Hell Raisers, unite," Blake whispered, waggling his eyebrows.

"That was ages ago," Marissa said, giggling. "We were so bad, like Fred and George Weasley."

I didn't say anything, even though everyone probably expected me to, because the Hell Raisers had been Blake's and my idea originally. I was up for pranking if that was what Blake had in mind. Reputation didn't really matter anymore, and if it did, there wasn't much I could do to recover mine: it was pretty much trashed. So I might as well have fun.

Charley cleared his throat in the silence and said, "We should have a movie night tonight."

"Yeah," Blake said. "I've got *Fight Club* and *Less than Zero* and *American Beauty*."

"*American Beauty* sounds good," Marissa said.

"You don't even know what it's about," I told her. "And you wouldn't like it."

"It's about a horse," Marissa said, and everyone burst out laughing.

"That's *Black Beauty*," I reminded her.

"Oh yeah."

"What about *Citizen Kane*? I have that," I suggested.

"I always fall asleep watching black-and-white films at night, though," Charley complained.

"Could you fall asleep watching *Sin City*?" Blake asked. "That's black-and-white."

"So's *Clerks*," Charley returned. "I meant old movies."

"So it seems we are at an impasse," I said.

"I just watched *Fight Club*. We might as well see *Less than Zero*. It'll keep Charley awake."

"Thanks, man," Charley said sarcastically. "I'm honored."

"What room are you in?" I asked.

"Milbank thirty-seven."

"We've got twenty-one," Marissa said.

"No shit, you got the huge corner room?" Charley asked.

"What a tragedy, right?" I rolled my eyes and tipped my water glass so that the last of the ice crunched in my mouth.

Later that night, armed with pouches of microwave popcorn, Marissa and I stepped out of our room and into the madness that was the second-floor Milbank hallway. Girls were hanging out in the hallway, eating candy, flipping through magazines, talking on their cell phones, and wandering in and out of their friends' rooms. I wasn't up for bonding with girls who made it abundantly clear by their dirty looks that they thought I mentally calculated the surface area of a penis before giving a BJ.

"Hi, Skylar," Alison Forsyth said sweetly, looking up from her stimulating literature of choice, a Delia's catalogue. She was wearing a Juicy Couture terry-cloth set and had replaced her contacts with glasses. "Not going to a boys' floor, are you?"

"Yes, my roommate and I are pumped to have wild sex all night long with some of those hot incoming freshmen," I said dryly. "You highly underestimate my prudence."

"I guess everyone underestimated you," she chirped, all sugar and carbs. "We didn't realize you were such a bitch. Ouch—it must suck to have everyone suddenly realize that you were the person ruining the curve all this time and pretending you didn't know who was doing it. You're going to be such a social leopard."

"You mean *leper*."

"You'd know." Alison arched an eyebrow at me.

Random fact: Alison Forsyth has hated me ever since freshman year, when she had the world's biggest crush on Kyle Dorsey, whom I was kind of hanging out with behind the boathouse. She was pissed when he invited me to the Graduation Gala, even if he claimed it was only "as friends," because, even though she'd never talked to him in her life, she was totally convinced he would ask her and then turn out to be a perfect gentleman. Sure.

I gave Alison one of my sweetest smiles, all Crest White Stripped and glossed to perfection, and said, "Why don't you just go shoot yourself in the head with a knife?"

It was classic, just like the cubic nonlinear Schrödinger equation.

Marissa and I stepped over Her Royal Heinous and made

our way to Blake's room. The four of us squeezed onto Blake's bed, with his iBook propped on a desk chair that had been dragged into the middle of the room. Somehow I wound up between Blake and Charley.

I tried to focus on the movie, but the problem was that it didn't remind me of the book. Books were more intimate. They didn't have director's cuts or deleted scenes. And how could anyone escape into a deleted scene with director's commentary?

On the screen, that dark-haired guy who looked like a young Johnny Depp was upside down in a little red car, singing. It seemed like something Blake would do.

I nudged him with my shoulder, but he got the wrong idea and stuck his hand on my leg, kneading my skin through the stretchy fabric of my yoga pants. It was so annoying, because I thought of Blake as my ex-boyfriend's kid brother, instead of an eligible Hilliard bachelor. Of which there were very few.

I glanced over at Charley, who had fallen asleep and was leaning against the wall, breathing deeply. His glasses were askew and the little nose pads had left angry red marks on the sides of his nose. I leaned over and gently plucked Charley's glasses off, placing them on the windowsill where he could find them easily when he woke up. Blake's hand was still on my leg.

"Do you mind?" I whispered, and he grunted and removed his hand, looking pissed off.

"Charley's asleep," I whispered.

"Charley's a pussy."

"Yeah, whatever. You totally degrade women, by the way, using that word."

"I'd call you a feminist, but isn't that word degrading, too?"

"Sure, Blake. It's the new f-word."

I smiled and Blake punched me in the shoulder and we were okay again, just old friends watching a movie about old friends. I turned my attention back to the movie. When the character Julian overdosed on whatever it was he was taking, and that Blair girl took care of him, I buried my head in Blake's shoulder, disgusted.

Why was it that boys who used drugs could never take care of themselves? They clearly didn't want to be rescued, so why put themselves in a potential rescue situation in the first place? They were like damsels in distress, only worse— dipshits in distress.

Thank God the DVD started skipping soon after the graphic drug scene, because I wasn't really interested in seeing how the movie ended.

When Blake went back to the menu to fix it, Marissa said, "I don't particularly want to watch this anymore."

So I said, "Motion to terminate watching of the film?"

"Second," Marissa called.

"There's a motion on the floor that's been seconded. All in favor?" I asked.

"Aye," we both said, before Blake had a chance to table the motion and get us back to the previously viewed scene, where we'd have been powerless to protest.

Blake obligingly flipped his laptop shut and we sat there on his bed in the semidark, because the door was propped.

Random fact: Hilliard had a rule that if there were members of the opposite sex in a dorm room, the door had to be open (and couples had to keep three feet on the ground). Stupid rule, I know, and I haven't always followed it. Study groups get loud, especially before finals when people like me are trying to study quietly. Plus how depressing is it to walk down a hall and see a group of students having fun in someone's room and know you weren't invited? I tried to point this out to Headmaster Bell last year, and he said rules are for the good of the governed, and I said what about Prohibition? How could Jews morally have Passover Seders? He said he understood why I was nationally ranked in Policy Debate.

While I thought about this, everything was quiet, so I said, "Why don't we bring back the Helliard Hell Raisers? It's the first night of summer session. Let's prank everyone to pieces."

"I call this meeting of Hell Raisers to order," Marissa said solemnly. "We've got Skylar, Blake, and myself in attendance, so that's a quorum. Charley can sleep."

" 'Ay, there's the rub,' " I joked, using my quoting voice. " 'For in that sleep of death what dreams may come?' "

"*Hamlet*," Marissa called.

"Soliloquy number?" I prompted.

"Sixty-nine?" Blake guessed sarcastically.

"Three," I told him, rolling my eyes. Was everything about sex with this kid?

Mental Lincoln-Douglas Debate: Is sex all boys think about? In the affirmative position, Skylar Banks. And to argue for the negative . . . anyone? Anyone at all?

I hiked my yoga pants back up my butt, where they were slipping down and threatening to give me a serious case of plumber's crack. Classy.

"So what do we do?" Marissa asked, eagerly planning the first Hell Raisers strike of summer session. She loved pranking. It was probably the only wholesome against-the-rules thing to do at boarding school.

"I thought up one prank, but we can't do it now," Blake said. "We get white crayons, right? And we put them next to the chalkboards, so the teachers think it's chalk, except whatever they write is permanent."

"That's good," I said. "We could definitely do that later. We need some sort of convocation prank, though."

"What about something with the computers?" Marissa asked. "We could change the AutoCorrect in Word to replace *however* with 'my teacher is a loser.' Like in the computer lab."

"Yeah," I said, "but no one has had any papers assigned yet. We need something people will notice."

"Like streaking," Blake added.

"You go do that," Marissa said. "We'll wait here."

Blake muttered and rolled his eyes.

Suddenly, I had it. A streak (pardon the pun) of brilliance.

"You guys!" I said. "The freshman scavenger hunt is tomorrow."

Actually, it was called CommUnity, where the whole Hilliard summer session community was invited to participate in a scavenger hunt during free period after lunch. Usually only freshmen were dumb enough to do it. I mean, why give up a perfectly good free period just to run around campus looking for a swan feather or whatever?

"Yeah, I'm looking forward to it," Blake deadpanned. "Bring on the FUnity."

"Not exactly," I said, more of the idea forming in my head as I talked. "You know how there are these really hokey items on the list? Why don't we add some fun stuff? Spice up the items?"

"Like a lock of hair from Headmaster Bell's toupee?" Marissa asked.

"Exactly!" I said.

"Well, where are we going to find this list?" Blake asked.

"It's always in the same place," I said, remembering. "Student Activities."

The Student Activities Office was in Reid Hall, one of the two main academic buildings.

"I have a key," Marissa said. She was president of the anime club.

"See?" I said to no one in particular. "It'll be easy. Like calculus."

Marissa checked her watch.

"It's ten-thirty," she informed us.

"Wanna meet outside our room at midnight?" I asked.

"The witching hour," Marissa breathed.

"Don't forget your invisibility cloak," I joked. "And Blake, try to wake Charley. It won't be fun without him."

4

Charley: Raindrops Are Falling on My Prank

As if everything wasn't royally screwed up enough, I woke up in Blake's bed. Blake was standing over me and waving a tiny airplane liquor bottle under my nose, which was not pleasant.

"Dude!" I sat up and ran a hand over my face. "Whuh . . . where did everyone go?"

"You fell asleep."

"Thank you, Professor Obvious."

"You fell asleep and everyone left," he clarified.

Smug bastard.

"So what happened?"

"Get dressed." Blake shrugged and flipped up the hood on his black sweatshirt.

"Wicked stealth hoodie," I muttered sarcastically, staggering to my feet. What time was it? Eleven-fifty. Damn, something was up.

"We're reinitiating the Hell Raisers tonight," Blake said, as I tugged on my own sweatshirt.

"No we're not," I said. "My parents will end me if I get in trouble."

"*I'll* fucking end you if you don't come with us," Blake said.

"Us?"

"The lovely ladies of Milbank twenty-one."

I stared at him. Skylar and Marissa were in on this, too? I couldn't say no if everyone else was committed. It wasn't just a Blake thing; it was the group.

I put on my glasses and flipped open my laptop.

> CharleyIIIOnGuitar: Skylar?
> MANO10 BLAHNIK: Zzzz. Oh wait, that's your line.
> CharleyIIIOnGuitar: Very funny. Hey, sorry I passed out during the movie.
> MANO10 BLAHNIK: Whatev. It wasn't a big deal. Hey, are you coming over?

Whoa. Did Skylar Banks just invite me to her room? Who knew that turning into Narcolepsy Boy made me an irresistible sex god?

> CharleyIIIOnGuitar: Coming over ;-)???
> MANO10 BLAHNIK: Yeah, with Blake. For the prank?

Oh.

> CharleyIIIOnGuitar: I guess I have to. But I'd rather not.
> MANO10 BLAHNIK: You know you want to have some fun. Come on. Please, Charley? For me?

CharleyIIIOnGuitar: OK. I'm in, but if we get in trouble, I'm going to claim that I was sleepwalking.

MANO10 BLAHNIK: I used that excuse last week when my dad got the credit card bill. I said I must've gone shopping on Amazon.com in my sleep. Didn't work.

CharleyIIIOnGuitar: Sounds crazy. Hey, I'll see you in a few.

MANO10 BLAHNIK: TTYL

I closed my laptop and pulled on my sweatshirt, leaving my own hood down.

"Ready to go?" Blake asked me, finishing the little liquor bottle and then tossing it into his trash can.

"That depends on what the prank is, and what it is you're doing."

"Relax, Charley boy. The girls thought this one up. We're 'improving' the FUnity scavenger hunt list. What I'm doing is pre-gaming."

A list? That didn't sound too bad. I could handle paper a lot better than, say, that time we'd put granny underwear on the bronze statue of Hilliard's first headmaster. I mean, if we got caught with handfuls of copies of the scavenger hunt list, what could our dorm parent do to us?

We walked over to Skylar and Marissa's room in the almost dark.

On the staircase, the safety floor strips lit up the wall, which had incredibly old photos on it of Hilliard Preparatory

School for Boys. Everyone looked so old-fashioned and severe in those photos, as though they called their fathers "sir."

There it was, above the second-to-the-bottom step: my dad's year. Sixty-eight. I could see him, staring solemnly at the camera, like he knew he was hot shit in his valedictorian shawl, on his way to Harvard pre-law, like he knew one day his son would stare at that very picture and feel inspired by how goddamn perfect his dad was. Bullshit. I wanted to rip the picture off the fucking wall and hang it in a community college somewhere just to piss my dad off.

"Dude, what gives?" Blake whispered, waiting for me at the bottom of the steps.

I sighed and followed him. We knocked softly on the girls' door. Skylar opened it and put her finger to her lips. She looked beautiful, and she wasn't wearing glasses like most of the girls do at night, after they took their contacts out. She had perfect vision. And a perfect GPA. Great.

We used one of the maintenance tunnels to get out of the dorms, and Skylar propped the door open using a stone someone had left at the end of the tunnel explicitly for that purpose.

As we snuck across the quad and into Reid Hall, I wondered if my dad had ever pulled any pranks at Hilliard. And then I wondered why I had even wondered something so impossible in the first place.

Skylar, Blake, and I waited outside Reid while Marissa slipped inside. The door to the building was never locked, although the individual rooms were. There was some superstition that you never prevented students from entering a place of learning, hence the unlocked door. I found this ridiculous. Seriously, how much learning has ever been done in the hallway?

Marissa came back out of the building after a minute. She had a thick stack of photocopied lists.

"Way to go," Skylar encouraged.

"Yeah, awesome," I added.

Blake scowled and lit a cigarette.

"Tobacco is wacko," Marissa told him, eyes twinkling, a smirk on her face. That girl had one weird sense of humor.

"Who gives a shit?" Blake asked.

"The lady in the poster with a hole in her throat, for one," Marissa shot back.

Blake shrugged and inhaled.

I watched the small bead of red light that illuminated the end of his cigarette as he inhaled. I wondered if it was ironic that a red light means stop. I wondered if Blake would care, and then I decided he definitely wouldn't.

By the time we got back to the second floor of Milbank, Blake had ditched his cigarette. I'd watched the red bead splutter and then die on the staircase, where Blake had left it for our dorm parent to puzzle over in the morning.

"Let me see the list!" Skylar said, trying to grab a copy from Marissa.

Marissa held them behind her and shook her head.

"Not yet. Charley, want to open a Word doc for us?"

I shrugged. I was sitting at Skylar's desk, and her computer was in front of me. I moved my finger over the touchpad of her PowerBook, exiting sleep mode.

"Can I read the list yet?" Skylar asked.

Marissa was about to hand it to her, but Blake snatched it from her hand.

"Sucka!"

"Whatever. Just read it," Skylar told him.

Blake cleared his throat and mock-pretentiously read, " 'Welcome to the eleventh annual CommUnity Hilliard Summer Session Scavenger Hunt! Use the items provided in your Scavenger Hunt Bag to accomplish the tasks, if needed. You have ninety minutes. Before the ninety minutes are up, your entire team needs to be back at the CommUnity table outside Reid. The team with the greatest number of items on the list and the fastest time wins fabulous prizes! Good luck, and ready, set go!' "

The list began:

- 1 set of plastic cutlery from McIntosh Dining Hall
- 1 photograph of a teacher flashing a peace sign
- 1 photocopy of every team member's Hilliard ID card
- 1 *Hilliard Howler* "Student Life" section with every word that starts with *h* highlighted.

We all laughed when Blake finished reading the rest of the list, not because it was a particularly humorous document, but because it was going to be.

Once we had a replica heading, we tackled the funny parts.

"Nothing too obvious," Skylar said, "or we'll be discovered too soon and the lists won't even be handed out."

"How about changing *annual* to *anal?*" Blake asked.

I dutifully typed it in. After a half hour, this is what we had:

Welcome to the eleventh anal CommUnity Hilliard Summer Session Scavenger Hunt! Use the items provided in your Scavenger Hunt Bag to accomplish the tasks, if needed. You have ninety minutes. Before the ninety minutes are up, your entire team needs to be back at the CommUnity table outside Reid. The team with the greatest number of items on the list and the fastest time wins absolutely nothing except a wasted free period! Good luck, and ready, set, go!

- 1 hairnet from McIntosh Dining Hall
- 1 photograph of a teacher flipping the bird
- 1 photocopy of every team member's butt
- 1 *Hilliard Howler* "Student Life" section with every word that has an odd number of vowels highlighted
- A photograph containing every member of the team's belly button (hint: get someone else to take it)
- An employee's tag from the student store
- A photograph of a team member putting a tampon in the Disaster Relief Fund donation box in the chapel
- Three photographs of three different locations in campus bathrooms where you can find rude graffiti (there are seventy-five locations in all)
- A piece of the bird poop coating the statue of Hilliard's first headmaster, Theodore J. Adams

"Oh man," I said, staring at a finished printout of the Eleventh Anal CommUnity list. "We're seriously going to do this?"

"It would be ridiculous to forget the whole thing now," Blake said. "Besides, it's *freshmen*."

"I guess."

Then I pictured the poor freshmen trying to convince a teacher to flip the bird for the camera, and I had to bust up laughing. We definitely had to do this.

So we printed up a bunch of copies.

"I'll take them back to Reid," Skylar volunteered, but then she grinned wickedly and said, "But only if Charley comes with me."

"Fine," I said, trying not to sound too excited that she had singled me out. Me! Not Blake.

I snuck a look at Blake. He scowled at me, and I shrugged. What can you do?

I took the copies and she took the key and we headed for the maintenance tunnel.

As we walked through the quad, there were about a million things I wanted to say to her. About how disappointed my parents had been when she won that award instead of me, about how I didn't really care, about how I wondered why I was even trying so hard, since I wasn't doing it for me. And then about how maybe one of the reasons I did still try, did still care, was because of her. I wanted her to notice me. I wanted to be good enough. And then there was the whole perfection thing everyone at Hilliard was so obsessed with. It was either 4.0 and Harvard or 2.0 and community college. B's didn't exist. In our world, there was no such place as a state school.

But then she looked at me and said the oddest thing.

"It's so half-assed, isn't it?"

"Isn't what?"

"You know. Summer session. It's like September's minor cousin. We move in, pomp and circumvention of dorm rules, whatever. But we don't mean it."

"We don't?"

"Of course not. Because we know summer session is temporary, only one class or two, just electives. So we don't try as hard. How many people did you see bringing dictionaries or printers with them today?"

I got what she was saying.

"No one, I guess." No one but her.

"But then in September?"

"Practically everyone."

"That's the thing, isn't it? In September, everything's permanent. Bad roommates, sucky dorm showers, oddly shaped rooms where you have to climb on your bed to reach your desk."

"Okay, so if right now doesn't matter, then why do we even bother?"

Skylar turned toward me, and I could see the moonlight casting shadows on her face, shifting through the trees, making her look haunted as she said, "Because we can't stop."

And then she smiled wryly, and the shadows made her even more beautiful.

"You can always stop," I said. "Just say no. Count to ten, get shipped off to a boarding school for bad rich kids."

Skylar snorted at the last one. There were two types of boarding schools: the kind for troublemakers, and the kind for kids who were openly hostile during National Honor Society student officer elections.

"But what if we can't stop?" Skylar pressed. "I'm serious. What if we've been studying for so long that we've become machines? And that's why we have summer session. It's like sleep mode, because if we shut down, for even one summer, we'd come back to school lazy and slow?"

"That won't happen. Not to us, anyway."

Skylar sighed. I saw the silhouette of her chest heave, and wondered if I could make her do it again.

"Sure it will. I was thinking today about when we came to Hilliard for the first time. I'd been totally goofing around with my friend Callie all summer, and then I got a B-plus on my first paper. I was rusty."

I hadn't known that. About the B-plus. I'd always thought of Skylar as perfect, above it all, better than the rest of us without even realizing it. But she realized it.

"It was a B-plus," I said. "Three years ago. It's not like you got a four on AP bio."

"Wait," Skylar said, grabbing my wrist. "You got a four?"

"It's no big deal," I said, shrugging, even though we both knew that Harvard only accepted fives for credit. But I wasn't really conscious of what I was saying. I was more conscious of Skylar's soft, warm hand around my wrist. No layers of clothing between us.

She let go of my wrist suddenly and I thought it was because she'd realized that she was touching me, a geek in a ratty Harvard sweatshirt and glasses, but then I realized we had reached Reid and she was just opening the door.

I had to squint when we got into the hallway so my eyes could adjust. Those twenty-four-hour lights were on, hidden behind metal grilles locked into the ceiling.

The building was amazing at night. It was just so calm and reassuring: the marble floor, the wood-paneled corridors, the wrought-iron staircase banister leading up to the second, third, and fourth floors in a squared-off spiral. I thought of all the famous alumni, and how they had studied in this building. I wondered if they'd ever snuck in late at night, the way my friends and I did.

Skylar didn't waste time. She opened the door of the Student Activities Office and whispered for me to drop the copies on the desk.

I did, and then, quickly, we closed the door and walked out of the building, trying not to laugh.

As we walked back to the dorms, I noticed that it had gotten darker outside. The moonlight was in splinters, coming and going as clouds messed around overhead.

I sniffed. It smelled wet.

"Skylar, you don't think it's going to rain, do you?"

She looked at me like she thought I was terribly funny, Mr. Hilarious, making a joke like that at one-thirty in the morning.

But then she looked up. I watched her tilt her head back, long dark hair glimmering.

"Shit, I think you're right," she told me.

And then she took my hand in hers and we ran back to the dorm laughing at the absurdity, laughing at the light drops that moistened our arms and legs and faces, laughing at the heavier drops that attacked just before we made it into the maintenance tunnel, laughing as we realized that the scavenger hunt was going to be canceled.

"If a prank is pulled but nobody discovers it," Skylar mused before Blake and I headed back to our own room, "does the prank exist?"

"Yeah," Blake said. "But then the prank's on us."

5

Skylar: To Hell in a Handbag

Mr. McCabe's classroom was an explosion of counterculture against the stately wood paneling and elegant leaded-glass windows. It was completely free of rows of desks, a fuzzy puppy calendar, Honor Code ditto sheets, a butcher paper sign hand-lettered with the school motto, or those annoying laminated posters of lily pads with motivational sans-serif script exclaiming how wonderful optimism is. In short, it was like nothing Hilliard had seen before.

Mr. McCabe was young enough that it made me wonder if he had just gotten his master's and transported the entire contents of his dorm room (furniture included) into his classroom. His posters were of CBGB's, *One Flew over the Cuckoo's Nest*, and Amnesty International. Bookshelves lined one wall and were crammed with J. D. Salinger and Hunter Thompson and Kurt Vonnegut.

All the desks were arranged in a circle, like in those support groups for women who can't cope with reading their ex-boyfriends' blogs. Not only did McCabe have bongo drums in his classroom, there was also a decrepit couch and a La-Z-Boy recliner in the back corner.

Just like in the MIT information session I went to last spring break, there wasn't one empty seat in Mr. McCabe's creative-writing class. After the first day, I'd started dressing up my uniform a little bit, and Mr. McCabe's class was fully giving me espadrille-from-hell and Ma-no-no Blahnik blisters.

On the third day of class, Marissa and I sat as close to McCabe as possible, so we could see the flecks of gold in his Gucci-green eyes. He was drop-dead-fall-off-your-platform-heels-in-shock gorgeous. Just one smile of his could capture the attention of every female student in the room.

" 'I am the master of my fate, I am the captain of my soul,' " Mr. McCabe said. "Who spoke those eloquent words?"

I could picture the book in my head, some anthology I'd flipped through. I thought about remaining quiet, but then I wondered what atrocities could possibly happen now if I answered the question, after I'd already been named senior honoree. So I raised my hand. Marissa stared at me in shock.

"Yes?"

"William Henley. 'Invictus.' "

"Right on!" McCabe said, giving the air a little punch with his fist. I took a deep breath and tried not to smile as he continued the lesson. "It was William Henley, a nineteenth-century English poet. But how many of you want to be the masters of your fate? Wouldn't you rather sit back and dream? Maybe those dreams will just come true on their own."

He paused and stared at us expectantly. The room was silent. We stared back at him, curious.

"Or maybe you already have a future. Law school! Partner before you're thirty! Following what everyone in your family has done since muttonchop whiskers made the ladies swoon."

Some giggling (aka swooning) from the class (aka the ladies) ensued.

"How about it? How many of you are content with what you've been given?"

Silence.

"Come on! We're talking about life here! The chance to make something of yourself. To have books written about you in languages that didn't yet exist when you were alive.

"And speaking of books and biographers, that brings us to today's assignment. Be the master of your fate. Captain your soul into the uncharted depths of your aspirations. And write an essay on anything you'd like, as long as the essay encapsulates you and tells me who you are. The only thing I ask is that you don't use the five-paragraph format. You need to express yourself in your own way. No introductory paragraph, no thesis statements. Forget all that and focus on the words. Bare your soul, be edgy, be daring, paint yourself as a character. Let the form come naturally. Length doesn't matter. And if you have questions later on, I'm going to give you my e-mail address. Don't hesitate to bother me. I teach summer school; I have no life."

Could he have taught any more like a college professor? Listening to him made me feel so grown-up, like he knew we were ready to graduate.

Well, maybe not all of us. I was worried about Blake. He

sat slumped a few seats away, gnawing on his pencil, smelling like the pot I'd seen him smoke behind the dining hall that morning. I'd totally caught him. I'd stepped behind the dining hall to smoke one of my cloves circle, and there he was, puffing on his little clay pipe like nobody's business.

I was all, "Blake, do you want to give me a light, or are you too busy trying to keep the munchies at bay?"

He reached into his messenger bag and rummaged around. I saw a bunch of bottles of prescription pills in there, which was strange, because Blake hadn't taken any meds during freshman year. He noticed me staring, so he turned his back to me and rustled through his bag until he found a flimsy matchbook. He tossed it to me, but by that time I was so over my clove. God. What was Blake doing with those pills?

"Are you a dealer?" I'd asked him, and he looked surprised and then laughed at me and said who did he know at Hilliard who would buy any shit off him?

"Whatever. Just make sure you get to class on time. And whatever's going on, Blake, I'm going to find out sooner or later."

Now I saw Blake remove the pencil from his mouth and lean over to tap Eunice Kim, aka one of the Kimchi Sluts, on the shoulder.

A little about the Kimchi Sluts: They were an inseparable trio of girls whose parents named them (oh God) Shirley, Eunice, and Doris. All of them had the same last name, although I didn't think they were related. They dressed spandex sexy and had matching belly button piercings and visible thong underwear with a string of crystal going up their butts.

The Kimchi Sluts wore glitter makeup and too much eyeliner, and everyone knew the stories of how Janice Weiner had broken up with her Farmington Prep "photographer" after some Groton guys saw him in a hot tub in Palm Beach with all three Kims over spring break. Random subfact: all three Kims had been topless in the tub, or so the rumor goes. I might have been a slut, too, but at least I'd never gone after anyone's boyfriend. What were they going to do, split him three ways?

So Blake was totally listening in on their conversation, and then he smiled and asked Eunice, "Are you talking about the party?"

I knew it was bad news if these girls were whispering about a party. This wasn't going to be one of those Pizza Hut affairs Ming Tsu and Ali Ahmad threw every quarter, trying to get people to join the Hilliard chess league.

Blake and the girls exchanged a few sentences, and then Blake leaned back in his chair, looking pleased. He caught my gaze from five chairs down and did one of those exaggerated winks, all goofy like he had been when we initiated the Hell Raisers two nights ago.

I watched Blake pull out his camera phone and take a picture of Doris's thonged ass crack. Blake had skipped straight over perv intro verse and gone straight to perv verse. Charley, across the circle with some of the Parli guys from debate, slipped his cell phone out of his pocket and stared at the display for a second in disgust as Blake shook with silent laughter.

After class got out, I tapped Marissa on the shoulder, because she didn't seem to realize we were free to go. She just sat there in class scribbling poems into her notebook. "Huh?" she muttered.

I leaned over her shoulder and read:

> I took the road most traveled,
> But I walked it by myself,
> Carefully sidestepping your footprints
> And tentatively stamping my own.
> Small steps, a swaggering strand,
> Alone
> Not Noah's ark, high heels cliquing
> Like you.

"Cool poem," I said, and Marissa slammed her notebook shut and blushed.

"Stop making fun of me," she said. "It's no good."

"It's really good," I said, shocked. "I mean it. Seriously. But whose footsteps were you side—"

"It's not important," Marissa mumbled, stuffing her notebook in her bag. "I'll catch up with you later."

She hurried out of the room with the rest of the students and left me standing there trying to figure out what she meant. When it was just Mr. McCabe and me, I felt the heavy strap of my bag dig into my shoulder and remind me of what I was about to do. He smiled. My heart fluttered like my eyelashes. I replayed the smile over and over in my mind as I shouldered my messenger bag and walked over to the desk, where he was gathering his stuff.

"Mr. McCabe?"

He removed a pen cap he'd been chewing on from the corner of his mouth.

"Yes, Shylar?"

"Skylar, actually," I corrected. Was it so hard to learn my name?

"Sorry. Skylar."

"It's fine," I said, in case he was worried he'd hurt my feelings. You know, because he was secretly in love with me and my achingly gorgeous shoe collection? "I was wondering, about the assignment? If we bare our souls, you're not going to tell Mr. Harcourt or anyone what we write?"

"Nope. The whole point in getting this class to think like adults is to treat you like adults. If you choose to write something in confidence, I'll keep it between us. I'm looking for content, not reason to commit you to therapy. If you want to be Susanna Kaysen or Augusten Burroughs, go ahead."

I smiled, and he smiled back.

"I'm not really a writer."

"Ah, you're one of those, Skylar?"

"What, a mathematician?" I asked.

"No. A writer who doesn't realize her own potential."

"I don't know about that. I'd rather read than write. I can imagine my life if I never wrote another word, but I can't imagine my life if I never read another book."

He leaned back in his chair and asked lazily, "Has it occurred to you during your extensive reading career that there are only a few stories to tell?"

"Kind of. I mean, I see patterns. It's like fractions. So many completely different fractions reduce into the same thing."

"Right on!" McCabe smiled. "Math is about figuring out what's the same, right? Reducing things? But English, literature, poetry, those noble pursuits are the search for difference. Everyone has their own unique lens through which they see the world. Ten men crossing one bridge is really ten men crossing ten bridges—have you heard that before? They all have different stories to tell about the same thing. You can reduce their stories to the crux, but when you do that, you miss the really good stuff."

"You're saying that nobody listens to stories, just storytellers?"

"Exactly!"

Did I dare write what I thought I was going to write for him? I still wasn't sure.

"Thanks. I never thought about it that way before. I have one more question, actually. Is this yours?"

I put a rumpled and rubber-banded manuscript onto his desk. The manuscript was by E. B. McCabe.

"Where did you get this?"

He picked it up and riffled through a couple of pages, and I wasn't sure suddenly if I had just done something completely stupid or a huge favor.

"It was on the floor in my mom's study. She's a literary agent. I had already signed up for summer session, and I recognized your name, so I thought . . ."

He stared at me. What had I thought? That he'd be happy

to have it back? That he'd want to sit down and discuss it and become, like, my mentor? That we'd sip hot chocolate in his office and debate who was the greatest writer of the twentieth century? That he would make me appreciate Proust, and I would show him the subtle joys of solving a mathematical proof?

He broke the silence by asking, "Is your mom Judy Banks?"

"Uh-huh."

"No kidding." He tossed the manuscript back onto the desk so the pages fanned across it. "I sent that a few months ago. She hated it. Yet another form rejection letter to add to my stack."

"Well, I liked it. Mr. McCabe, I hope you don't mind, but I read your manuscript and it rocked. Very much a cross between Salinger and Kerouac. Possibly even with an S. E. Hinton vibe thrown in."

"Really? You know, Skylar, I don't think I've ever talked with anyone who's read my stuff before. You're not playing around? You liked it?"

"Yeah, totally. That one part—page seventy-three, I think it was: 'No matter how screwed up your life is today, today is just a collection of moments that stop and start where you want them to. And nothing upsetting matters when you know that tomorrow's gonna be better than yesterday.' That was my favorite part. When the guy didn't worry so much anymore about people finding out his problems, and he started doing what he wanted instead of what everyone expected."

"You memorized it?"

"It's not a big deal. I memorize quotes a lot for debate."

Anyway, I'm sorry my mom rejected your manuscript, but I think she was the wrong agent for it. She doesn't handle coming-of-age, or anything gritty, really. Just celebrity biography and commercial fiction."

"Huh." Mr. McCabe folded his arms and shook his head, chuckling.

"What?"

"I can't wait to read whatever it is you're going to write for me, Skylar Banks. I have a feeling it won't be like anything I've seen before."

"I'll try not to disappoint," I said.

"What's up, beautiful?" Blake asked, arching an eyebrow. He'd been waiting for me outside the door to McCabe's room.

"Well, that depends," I said, "because if by 'up' you mean 'high,' that would be you."

"Don't you have a math book to memorize?" he countered.

Weak. Very weak. I'd say I won that round of Mental Sparring Match, but I'd be merciful and let him break to the next round.

"Yeah, maybe. So what's the *deal*?"

"I'm not a dealer."

"Okay. Jeez. Don't get your tighty-whities all up your crack about it."

"So anyway. There's this party tonight. Schwartz Theater, pretty good liquor, I heard. Catcher Yee got a fake ID. I'm inviting you."

"Let's see it." I stuck out my hand.

"See what?"

"The invitation."

"Uh, this is the invitation. You know, I ask you if you want to come, and then you tell me your decision."

"Oh. Well, I thought that since you were lording it over me, there was going to be a fancy paper invite. Or at least a sort of plus-one thing going on. But obviously it's just an open house and anyone can show, so you don't need to invite me."

"Smartass," Blake muttered, taking a box of spearmint Tic Tacs out of his pocket and dumping a small white one into his fist. Funny, I thought spearmint was supposed to be green.

"Well, since I clearly don't need to RSVP through you, let's just say that I may or may not show up tonight. The same goes for Marissa. I might rather, oh, I don't know, memorize a math book?"

Blake had already swallowed the Tic Tac, which I thought was odd. We walked to the dining hall in silence, and halfway through Brooks Quad, I realized what was up. Blake hadn't taken a Tic Tac. It had been a pill.

Suddenly I didn't know what was going on with him anymore. He didn't seem like the same guy from freshman year, the crazy fourteen-year-old goofball who had passed out condoms after chapel on Talk Like a Pirate Day, because "the campus was filled with seamen." He was darker, almost. More jaded. Less flashy, even. And it worried me.

6

Charley: Gin, Rum, Me

In eleventh grade I was voted president of the drama club because I thought up the best T-shirt slogan: "May the Schwartz be with you."

On the front, there was a picture of two cloaked dudes battling it out with light sabers, like in the Mel Brooks farce I got the slogan from, *Spaceballs*. One wore a sad-face drama mask and the other wore a happy one. The back read, "Schwartz Theater Players, Hilliard Preparatory School."

I was wearing this shirt and my boxers, lying in bed and reading *The Amazing Adventures of Kavalier & Clay*, which Skylar had loaned me at lunch while we were discussing McCabe's essay. I turned a page and glanced at the clock. It was after lights-out, eleven-thirty almost, and I was using my flashlight.

Suddenly Blake's wristwatch alarm went off and he sat up in bed.

"Got a hot date?" I asked him as he rubbed at a pillow crease on his cheek.

"Yeah, with Jack Daniel's."

"Dude, you have no idea how wrong that sounds."

Blake grunted, and I watched him get up and put on his navy blue Yale sweatshirt and a pair of jeans.

"Where are you going?" I asked.

"It's not where I'm going, it's where *we're* going."

"No way, Blake." I put my book down and shone the flashlight up in his face.

"Suit yourself," he said, squinting. "Let Skylar think you're such a loser you won't even come to a party in Schwartz Theater."

"Skylar's coming?"

I lowered the flashlight as I had a mental panic attack: Skylar and I were close now, like we'd been freshman year. But girls were fickle; they changed their minds as often as they changed handbags. Maybe she'd be at that party, waiting for me, and when I didn't show, she'd hang out with Blake instead of me, and maybe she'd like Blake better. Don't girls like bad boys? Or how about another guy, like Pete "Sticks" Donahue, who won state for Parliamentary Debate, or Hunter Chaffee, who didn't need to ask, "Do you know who my father is?" because it was always just understood? If Skylar was going to this thing, I had to go so she'd keep on liking me. It was such a goddamn stupid reason, though.

"Dude, I asked if Skylar was coming," I reminded Blake.

"Well, I invited her. If she asks where you are, I can always say you were off with Alison Forsyth, y'know, since she and Skylar are buddies."

Meaning Skylar thought Alison was a bitch.

"Okay, I'll go. But I'm not getting trashed. Morning chapel's bad enough without a hangover."

I put on the jeans that were draped across the back of my chair. Since it was a party, I put on one of my uniform oxford-cloth shirts, but untucked and not all annoying-looking. Then I thought maybe I should tuck it in, but then it looked stupid and puffy that way, so I untucked it again.

Blake lit a cigarette, so I took my time rolling my sleeves, because I remembered a few years ago when Skylar had told me she thought it looked sexy. She hadn't said "sexy," though. She'd said "cute." I hated that word. Cute. Puppies are cute, I'd told her, not shirtsleeves.

"Do we need the flashlight?" I asked Blake.

"Nah. Leave it," he said, tossing the butt of his Parliament out the window.

As we snuck across the quad, Blake said, "This is going to be so fun, man. You have no idea."

Fun. There was a word I didn't use often—when would I? SATs are fun? International Extemporaneous Debate is fun? My GPA is fun? My parents are fun? Come on.

But Blake seemed to be having the time of his life. He was the master of his fate and the captain of his soul.

"Yeah," I said. And then, "Hey, Blake? Why did you leave Hilliard?"

"Why do you want to know?"

"No reason. You just seem to like it, so I was wondering why you left."

"My parents went through that midlife crisis thing, where they realized their boys were all grown up. They wanted me home, so I went."

"Midlife crisis," I echoed, but I was thinking about an article I'd cited in one of my speeches on intellectual property rights. It said something about Mike Dorsey, Blake's dad. I couldn't remember exactly, but it sounded like after he sold his company, he had to pay a lot of the money to the guy who held a patent on something, and he went to court and lost basically everything. I'd thought the article was just talking about shareholder stuff, but then I wondered if maybe it had been bigger than that.

"What's the problem, Charley boy?" Blake asked, sounding kind of pissed.

"Nothing. I just don't want to get in trouble."

"Have I ever gotten you into trouble?" Blake demanded.

"Not really," I said. But he had gotten me into trouble all the goddamn time freshman year, I realized. That time my parents came up for parents' weekend and they smelled smoke on my uniform and took away my text messaging for a month. Or when Blake Saran Wrapped my laptop shut as a joke but then he left the window open and the heat shrank the Saran Wrap so we couldn't get the plastic off and I ended up having to run to the computer lab to write my essay. Or when Blake stashed a *Playboy* in my debate files and Coach found it when he was showing me how to color-code my articles by world issue.

Schwartz Theater loomed ahead, the second-tallest building on campus (the tallest was the chapel, because of the cupola with the bells). Schwartz was the perfect place to party. It was near the dining hall and the chapel, which were closed most of the time. A quad and a half from the teachers' offices, far enough from the dorms, and practically on the opposite side of campus from the faculty housing.

Blake slipped around to the back of the theater and I followed him, nervously playing with the bottom button of my untucked shirt. What if one of the dorm parents was waiting for us inside, ready to write "community college" across our transcripts?

"Hey," Janice Weiner called from just inside the dressing area backstage. She handed us empty red plastic cups.

"Thanks," I said. Was that stupid? Were you supposed to thank people for that sort of thing, or just accept the cup with a cool nod like you were expecting it?

Blake nodded and gave Janice a big hug. Why was it that some guys could get away with hugging girls hello and goodbye like it was no big thing, while I freaked out when Skylar touched my wrist?

There were about forty people inside. The prop table was covered with half-empty bottles of Jägermeister and Grey Goose and Absolut and Skyy. Some beers, some wine coolers and hard lemonade.

The set from the last play of the year, *Rumors*, was pretty much intact. It was comical, almost, to see all the National Merit Scholars lounging around on beautifully upholstered armchairs and spooning on a settee beneath framed artwork. There was this weird house party vibe from the set, not like I'd ever been to a house party.

But these kids definitely had. They were the "cool" nerds,

the 4.0 students who were always talking about how they got "so trashed, man, you have no idea" whenever they weren't studying or winning sports trophies. They got their friends who lived nearby to sign them out overnight on weekends and then had blowout parties in nearby mansions. Their parents didn't seem to care what they did so long as they kept up their appearances and grades. My parents would freak out if I got contact lenses. In short, there was no "cool" before my nerd label. And whatever, I was fine with that. At least I wasn't going to have to take my college finals with a wicked bad hangover every semester.

I watched Blake pour himself a helluva lot of Jack Daniel's and tip the cup back, downing it all in one shot. All I wanted was a shot at valedictorian.

"Have fun." Blake winked at me, abandoning the cup and taking the bottle with him as he walked over to chill with Shirley, Eunice, and Doris, who were giggling in a corner and wearing shorts so small and tight that they looked like bathing suit bottoms.

I looked around, the play set confusing me, making me think I should be reciting lines, facing the audience, and looking for my dad in the back row before stepping out of who I was to become some character who always knew what to say and where he'd wind up. Shrugging off the weirdness, I followed Blake to see what was going on.

The Kim chicks were pink-faced and looked kind of trashed, but maybe they knew where Skylar was. I thrust my hands in my pockets and tried to look like I abandoned my SAT prep to get wasted every night of the week.

"Is my face red?" Eunice wanted to know.

Doris and Shirley giggled.

"Is it?"

One of the girls handed her a tiny mirror.

"Oh my God! It totally is."

"So I'm guessing you've had a lot, then." Blake smirked.

"Hey, you're, like, Kyle Dorsey's brother, right?" Shirley asked.

"Yeah. Blake."

"I'm Charley," I said. I should have said, *Hi, I'm a debate geek who followed his roommate to a party and now I have no idea what to do with myself except try not to look down your tops.* That might have been more accurate.

Shirley patted the floor next to her and Blake sat down.

"Um, have you seen Skylar?" I asked.

"No, maybe she's, like, studying particle physics and then doing it on a lab table." Doris laughed evilly.

"Yeah, man," Blake said sharply to me, "why do you care so much? You're obsessed with her, dude."

"I'm not . . . it's . . . uh, later," I said brightly, wandering back to the drinks table and looking around. Skylar wasn't there. Neither was Marissa; not like I'd expected Marissa to be chugging a beer and then dancing on the props table, but still. It was just Blake and me, and suddenly not even Blake, who had his arm around a very red-faced Doris Kim.

What was I doing there? I took one last look at Blake, who was chugging JD while the girls giggled. I was gone.

It was depressing walking back to the dorm by myself, knowing that I'd gotten so worked up over a stupid party and then left after five minutes. When I slipped back into my room,

I turned on my flashlight and reached for my guitar. I needed to play for a while to calm down. With no amp and a T-shirt under the door, I could strum the strings as hard as I wanted.

I bent over the fretboard and pummeled my way through "Highway to Hell." I did all the AC/DC I knew, and then I was just strumming chords, making stuff up, frustrated. Why couldn't I just enjoy myself? Was it so hard to relax? I just wanted to get to Harvard already so my parents would lay off. So they'd be proud.

So my class picture could hang over the dorm stairs with me in the valedictorian shawl like my father had been. Maybe the photos would hang directly across from each other, and my eighteen-year-old dad and eighteen-year-old me would be locked in an eternal staring match, neither of us able to blink.

I tossed my Fender medium-thick pick across the room and heard it clatter to the floor somewhere near Blake's desk. Then I sat down at my own desk and did the worst thing imaginable: I started my homework.

It was a quarter till midnight and I opened my laptop and started typing a header for my creative-writing assignment. If I got the whole thing done that night, I could do another SAT practice test the next day.

Charley Morton
Creative Writing
Essay #1
Perfect Pick

I found a guitar pick in my jeans pocket yesterday. It was pearly white and had the convex center from where I had sucked it too hard while finger-picking. The bottom point was rounded into a little half-moon, from being dragged over metallic strings and made to sing. I ran it between my fingers and felt the small bumps on its plastic surface. I remembered this pick.

When I was twelve my mother took me into the music store near Harvard Square and I saw the guitar I had to own. Black and white, gleaming under the fluorescent lighting of the "do not touch" display. It had a red leather strap and six sharp strings begging to ripple under my thumb. I asked her for it, but she shook her head. Electric guitars were for rock stars, she said. Stoners, high school dropouts, not future doctors. What she meant was, not for me. Instead my mother bought me the awkward, bulky acoustic that was on sale, and said I could use it to play classical music in Hilliard's Classical Ensemble in a few years. It didn't have metal strings to make crisp music, but clumsy plastic strings that looked and sounded like yarn. This wasn't my guitar. It couldn't be. But there it sat, in a vinyl case, on the floor of my bedroom. I wouldn't touch it.

After a week my curiosity got the best of me and I opened up the guitar's case. I found myself staring at the perfect pearly white pick, wedged underneath the high E string. I cradled the ugly guitar to my chest and dragged the pick back and forth, back and forth. I wasn't playing the guitar—I was molding my pick for when I got the chance to play the black and white electric.

A month before I turned thirteen, I couldn't stop jabbering about the black and white guitar. It was a huge surprise when, instead of a set of encyclopedias or a leather desk set, my parents gave it to me on my birthday. The one condition was that I could only play once I had finished my homework, and only for fun. No bands, serious jam sessions, or playing for money in a T station over the summer. I didn't care. I ran to my room and retrieved the white pick from my sock drawer. It rippled over the taut metal and each note rang at its zenith, tumbling back into the tablature of *Beginning Rock Songbook I,* a secret possession of mine. The pick became my personal good-luck charm.

When I was fourteen, I signed up for a guitar competition, the Riff-Off—a chance to solo in front of my entire middle school. My lucky pick against my thumb, I started nervously with a G sus seven. Music's sweet tune poured out of the five amplifiers and crashed to a halt as I began to stumble. The pick betrayed me, vibrating with a will of its own across the wrong strings.

After everyone clapped to be nice and I was through being embarrassed, I put that pick in my pocket and swore I'd never pick up the guitar again as long as I lived. My parents had seen me fail. They'd given up their evening plans just to watch their son make a gigantic mistake, and I could sense their disappointment in me. But even though I'd screwed up, I couldn't stop myself from playing. I brought

INSTANT MESSAGE FROM MANO1O BLAHNIK: ACCEPT? DECLINE? BLOCK?

I hit Accept and entered the chat.

MANO1O BLAHNIK: Hey, how was the party?
CharleyIIIOnGuitar: Crap. I stayed five minutes. Blake seemed to enjoy himself, though.
MANO1O BLAHNIK: He's not with you?
CharleyIIIOnGuitar: No. Why?
MANO1O BLAHNIK: Do you know what time it is???
CharleyIIIOnGuitar: Shit! Two o'clock.
MANO1O BLAHNIK: He knows campus rules. He's only ever out after midnight if we're pranking, but never this late, and never alone. Something's wrong. I can feel it. We should check it out.

I sighed. Perfect. This was just perfect. Because of Blake I'd be sneaking out twice in the same night. It was late, and Blake had looked pretty serious about getting wasted.

CharleyIIIOnGuitar: Yeah. Let's do it.

MANO10 BLAHNIK: Meet at the downstairs drinking fountain in five minutes?

CharleyIIIOnGuitar: I'll be there in two.

Marissa and Skylar were already at the drinking fountain when I got there. Skylar led the way through the maintenance tunnel by the light of her cell phone. We kept quiet until we reached the theater. Backstage, the lights were off and it was quiet. There wasn't any muffled music or talking or laughter. The party was clearly over.

Although someone had tried to clean up a little, there was a stain on one of the armchairs that smelled strongly of 80 proof, and a scattering of Altoids had spilled into the crevices between the floorboards. The furniture was askew and some cups were wedged between the sofa cushions. Everyone had left. But where the hell was Blake?

"He's here, I know he is." Skylar looked worried.

"Maybe he was kidnapped and stranded in a cow pasture fifty miles from here." Marissa's eyes were wide. Yeah, as though that was what happened. Maybe Obi-Wan had hacked off all his limbs with a light saber. Or maybe Voldemort got to him.

I looked around. That was when I noticed that one of the doors to a dressing room was ajar. I walked over and flipped on the light.

An empty bottle of Jack Daniel's was next to a trash can that stank like vomit. Lying on the linoleum, shit-faced, was Blake.

I'd never seen someone passed out before. He was passed out, wasn't he?

I nudged Blake's side with my shoe. He didn't groan. Didn't move. *Oh shit.*

I was so freaked out that I backed away, right into someone. Skylar.

"Sorry," I mumbled.

"Never mind. We need to deal with this," Skylar said, tying her hair back from her face with an elastic. Her eyes looked huge and beautiful and green. She grabbed my hand and squeezed. And I knew there was no one I'd rather have to handle this with than her.

"Come on." She got down on the floor and patted Blake's cheek. "Wake up!"

He didn't move. She rolled him over. There was still some vomit on his chin. I dug in my pocket and handed Skylar a tissue to clean it off.

She winced as she tossed the tissue into the trash can.

"Ugh. That smells so foul."

Marissa made a little noise from the doorway.

"What did he take?" Marissa asked, and I looked at her with surprise.

"As far as I know, just a lot of Jack Daniel's."

"Oh. But he's breathing, right? He's only . . ."

"Passed out," Skylar and I both said at the same time.

"Damn this," Skylar said. "We're going to have to carry him back to the dorm."

I sighed. At least I'd already rolled up my sleeves.

"He's not going to barf on me, is he?" I asked.

"No, I think he got most of it out of his system," Skylar said. "Try to get him upright—here, shove!"

I thought we'd never get Blake back to the dorm. I felt like a murderer, dragging his body through the quads, practically across the entire campus. Marissa wasn't much help. She hovered toward the back, afraid to touch Blake, muttering about cow pastures or something. Skylar groaned under the weight but didn't complain. I thought that was awesome. How many girls will drag a passed-out boy across two acres without bitching about how they broke a nail?

Marissa at least used her cell phone to light up the maintenance tunnel. Finally we got to the third floor.

"Come on, almost there," Skylar encouraged, little wisps of light brown hair dangling loose from her ponytail in front of her eyes.

At last we dumped Blake on his bed, placing him on his side with the trash can right beside him.

It was over. I stood there, sweating, at three in the morning, uncaught, too alert to sleep, and unsure of what to do next.

"Do you want us to stay?" Skylar asked, placing her hand on my shoulder. I could feel the heat of her skin through my thin oxford-cloth shirt.

"I don't want you to leave," I said, hoping that was an okay answer. Did she want to stay because of me, or because of Blake? I hoped it was me she was breaking dorm rules for.

All I knew was that I'd be awake until morning and I could use some company. Otherwise I'd wind up staring at

Blake for hours making sure he didn't choke on his own vomit. Delightful.

"So we'll stay," Skylar said.

"Yeah, definitely," I said.

Skylar rummaged through my Dopp kit for some Tylenol and placed them and a half-empty water bottle on the windowsill at the head of Blake's bed.

Then she sat down on my bed and Marissa curled up in my desk chair. Marissa grabbed one of the *Watchmen* comics off my desk and turned on my flashlight to read. Guess she wasn't feeling social.

Skylar and I stretched out foot to head. I tossed her a pillow, and she giggled and poked me in the ribs with her big toe. There was a tiny flower painted on her toenail.

"So," Skylar said, "how's the SAT prep going?"

"Fine. I'm tanking the math, though."

"By tanking you mean seven-eighty?"

"I wish."

"Still. I don't see why you care so much. It's not going to make a difference anyway between early decision Harvard and early decision Harvard."

"It matters to me."

"It doesn't matter to you, Charley." She sighed. Her chest heaved. It was glorious. "It matters to your parents."

"Same difference."

"No, not same difference. You're a person, aren't you? You need to let them know. Unless you want to be Dr. Charles Morton the Third."

"That's the thing," I said. "Not really. I wish my parents could have seen me handle Blake tonight. I was clueless. Maybe then they'd change their minds. I'm not even that good at science or math, but I don't have a choice."

"You do! Charley, you read books. You give speeches. You don't have to be a doctor. But you're going to, because your parents are assholes."

"Skylar!" I nudged her shoulder with my foot.

"What? I can't say it? So let's just say you aren't valedictorian."

"That means you would be."

"This isn't about me," Skylar said, sitting up and getting really into the conversation. "What will they do to you?"

"Shit, who knows? Psychoanalyze me? Sue me? What can they do?"

"That's the point, Charley. They can't do anything to you, and they can't make you do anything."

"Yeah?"

"Yeah. What do you want to be when you grow up? Say we turn communist and everyone is paid the same, and Harvard is no more prestigious than community college. What job would you want?"

"What job would *you* want?" I challenged.

"Easy. I'd be a college professor of mathematics or I'd put together the outfits for shows like *Sex and the City*, if that was still on TV. Now you."

"I'd play guitar. But that's stupid."

"It's not."

"Yeah, it is. I have to make a living."

"What, so you can send little Charles Morton the Fourth to Hilliard and expect him to be valedictorian, too?"

"Hell no."

We laughed and poked at each other with our toes.

"Can I at least hear you play?" Skylar asked.

I didn't really play for other people, not since the Riff-Off incident, but I couldn't say no to Skylar. And part of me had hoped that one day I wouldn't be playing just for myself anymore, but for someone who actually wanted to hear my music.

I swung my legs over the side of the bed, reaching for my guitar and taking the pick out from underneath the high E string. I took my capo off the first fret and checked the tuning with a tentative strum.

I played some Springsteen, and Skylar scooted up next to me. I could feel her thigh pressing against mine while my fingers pressed against the strings, bumping the fretboard with each chord change. It was goddamn perfect, if I didn't think about Marissa reading at my desk and Blake completely intoxicated four feet away.

When I finished the song, Skylar took the guitar from me and laid it across her lap.

"You can really play," she said. "I mean it. It's like you lose yourself in the music."

She closed her eyes. She was so close to me that I could see the little creases on her eyelids where her eye shadow had gathered and made dark lines.

For some reason, I was almost positive she had stayed because of me, and I knew it was all right then to turn toward her, our faces inches apart, and whisper, "I didn't lose myself, I found you."

"Do you remember freshman year?" Skylar asked suddenly, shifting away from me on the bed, making me feel like an idiot for thinking I knew what was going on in her mind before.

"Best year of my life. I finally got away from my parents. I met you guys. There was no PSAT and no APs."

"We started the Hell Raisers. I didn't have such an awful reputation." She glanced warily at Blake before adding, "From getting caught fooling around with Kyle."

"It's not so bad," I said.

"You're right. It's not like I blogged my R-rated pics or something."

"At least it isn't true."

"How do you know?" Skylar raised an eyebrow suggestively and licked her lips.

"Stop that," I ordered. "You're creeping me out."

Actually, she was turning me on, and subsequently, I was thinking of turning on my computer. Ah, the miracle of Google.

We both laughed then.

"What are you going to do for college?" I asked her.

"MIT."

"You're crazy."

"Nope, I'm just trying to re-create *Good Will Hunting*," she joked.

"Because I can picture you as a janitor," I said sarcastically.

"What? The keys will totally match my Prada bag," she said.

I've always thought it would be so cool to just look at math and get it, you know? Not have to struggle to understand or study to do well.

"What's it like?"

"I don't know. Maybe like . . . like I should know the answer to every question, like I have to know it. Sometimes it feels too easy, like I don't deserve things. Like in debate? For me speech is just a matter of plugging words and statistics into a formula. All I have to do is quote articles I've skimmed and remember dates. That's the only reason I win. You're a better public speaker. You have way more stage presence than I do. I remember that one time—"

"You remember everything," I half teased.

"I know. But I'd rather not."

Blake started snoring loudly from his bed. I looked over at him, and then back at Skylar with a small smile, because I found snoring hilarious. But Skylar wasn't smiling.

She looked serious as she said, "I just wish it was freshman year all over again and nothing like this had happened yet."

And for one glorious moment, girls weren't a mystery, because I knew exactly how Skylar felt.

7

Skylar: Dorm Room of Ill Repute

After staying up till three and then crashing in the guys' room, I could barely stay awake the next day. But I can't stand being unproductive, or wasting time, so while Marissa spent free period napping, I sat on my bed wearing pajama bottoms and a tank top and drifting in and out of those online logic and probability forums.

I clicked into my favorite forum, which was usually full of difficult stuff. But the new teasers were easy, beginners' stuff like where three missionaries and three cannibals need to get across a river on a boat, but there can never be more missionaries than cannibals in any position. Not like I'd want to be in the missionaries' position. Ha ha ha.

Sighing with boredom, I pulled up a Word doc and stared at the blinking cursor. It was like I had to write about it. My reputation, I mean. Or how I got it. So I titled it "Dorm Room of Ill Repute," and wrote:

What do I remember about freshman year? It was boarding school for the first time and I was so unsure about everything, really, except that I'd gone to get away from the suburbs I'd never wanted to live in anyway. The first day I must've spent an hour getting ready before breakfast, flat-ironing my hair, staring at my uniformed reflection in the mirror, decorating my binder with photographs of my friends and me so everyone could look over at my desk and see how cool I was. How did I know that no one cares in board-ing school—that you aren't supposed to try hard to be cool, but embody this quality without effort? That the only "cool" photos aren't cool at all but standard shots of friends on ski vacations and in swimming pools of luxe country homes, rather than goofy pics in oversized sunglasses at the drugstore, or in the Barnes & Noble café.

Breakfast was strange, eating with hundreds of other students in a dining hall instead of eating a Pop-Tart in the car. There were cafeteria table cliques even at breakfast, but none of the fresh-men knew each other. I took my bowl of cereal over to a table where there was a cute guy with floppy blond hair and sat down across from him. He was reading a paperback novel.

"*The Rules of Attraction*," I read out loud. He looked up and smiled.

"Do you like Bret Easton Ellis?"

"Uh . . . ," I stalled, trying to think of something that would sound intelligent yet flirty. "I personally can't believe the way he wrote all those books when he was so young. Practically our age. Could you imagine finishing pre-calc homework and then working on a novel?"

"Exactly!" He smiled again, the cutie in the polo shirt without a popped collar. "I know what you mean. It would be wicked crazy."

"Totally. I'm Skylar, by the way."

"Charley. So, Skylar, you like to read?"

"Yeah. I wish I had more free time, though. I used to be such a bookworm when I was younger."

"I did, too. I spent a whole summer immersed in Tolkien when I was twelve."

"Wow, so did I!"

"Crazy."

We sat there in silence for the next few minutes, eating. Charley bookmarked his page and put the book into his North Face backpack.

"Can I see your schedule?" I asked.

"Yeah, sure." He took it out of his pants pocket and slid it across the table.

"Wow, you're taking French *and* Latin? Why would you do that to yourself? It's madness."

Charley rolled his eyes and took a sip of orange juice.

"My parents. They say I have to take both to be competitive for Harvard, and if I feel like it junior year, I can start Spanish or German as well."

"Jeez, are you good at languages or something?"

"I dunno. Probably not. But I taught myself how to write in Elvish after reading *Lord of the Rings*."

"That's sad."

"Yeah, I know." He chuckled. "Well, now I get to see your schedule. Fair's fair."

I opened my purple binder, the one with my schedule hole-punched neatly in front of the first tabbed divider.

"Is this right?"

"Uh-huh," I told him, tucking my hair behind my ears. "Why?"

"It says honors pre-calculus. Are you really taking that?"

"Yeah, why?"

"It's not normal for a freshman. You're unbelievably advanced. That class is gonna kill you."

"Probably, but failing's half the fun."

"Try telling that to my parents."

"Fine, I will. Call them up."

"You're joking, right?"

"Oh, you never know with me." I saw a lot of the students returning their trays and heading for chapel.

"Sit with me in chapel? Then we can get lost finding English class together afterward."

"Sure, just a sec." Charley shoved a large spoonful of soggy cereal into his mouth and chewed vigorously. "Okay, lead the way, O Captain, my Captain."

"*Dead Poets Society.*"

"Ungh! Incorrect. The right answer is: Walt Whitman."

"Well, yeah, but it was in *Dead Poets Society.*"

"Do I sense a debate coming on?"

"Only if you're prepared to lose. I'm going to kick your *aff*," I joked, then mentally groaned. God, I was such an idiot, making debate jokes.

"If that's your contention, it's wicked weak."

We laughed. It was a relaxed laugh, the kind that you sometimes do when you click with a person you've just met and can't believe you'd never spoken to them, like, an hour ago.

"Skylar, over here!"

That was Marissa, my roommate and book swap buddy in first-period English, waving me over to a seat in the front row.

I shrugged, grabbed Charley's wrist, and dragged him to the front row as well. Unfortunately, that was Mrs. Forrest's class.

Mrs. Forrest, or, as the upperclassmen snickeringly called her, Mrs. Rain Forrest, had a bit of a problem with her talk spittle. Okay, actually, the woman spit saliva through her teeth. When her mouth was closed, I could still feel Essence of English Teacher raining down upon me. But the seating chart stuck for the rest of the year, trapping us in the wet zone.

On that first day, there was a boy sitting behind us who I thought was even cuter than Charley, with curly hair and long eyelashes that just weren't fair. He didn't have to spend $20 a tube for Chanel Ultra-Lash.

Five minutes into the period, he tapped me on the shoulder. I turned around, and he tipped his spiral notebook so I could read it: *Weather forecast: RAIN!!!*

I couldn't help but laugh. Blake made me laugh a lot that year. He took to humming "Singin' in the Rain" whenever we walked into class.

I had two of my classes with Blake: English and Spanish. Charley and Marissa were only in my English class. We all wrote for the school paper that year, under Mrs. Rain Forrest's orders. I got to be one of the assistant copy editors, because my mom had taught me all of those fancy editing marks. Charley used to call the stack of edited articles on my desk the "comma sutra," which made Marissa blush once we explained the joke.

I guess I clung to Marissa as a friend that

year because it's hard for me to find friends that are girls. I'm better with boys. Marissa was okay because she was simply sweet and quiet. And quiet was good because Blake and Charley and I never seemed to shut up.

Blake had this brother in the school, Kyle, a senior. He came and knocked on Blake's door one day when we were all having an English review session in the room. The second I saw him, I swear to God, I almost swallowed my tangerine Altoid. Stunning. He was wearing a muddy lacrosse uniform with a C on the chest, and stuck his head into the room right after he knocked.

"Blake, goddamn!" He slammed his fist against the door again.

"What?" Blake asked.

Kyle came in, sat on Blake's bed, and tossed a piece of paper onto the floor.

"Are you serious?" Blake scanned the paper. "This is a forgery, right?"

"Nah, bro, that's the real deal. It is a bona fide unconditional early action acceptance letter to Yale *fucking* University!"

"Yale?" Charley joked. "But of course Yale was your safety if you didn't get into Harvard."

Kyle smiled. "Look, kid, there are two types of people at this school: Yale-Harvard guys and Harvard-Yale guys. I am of the former preference."

"So you prefer guys, you're saying?" I joked.

Everyone groaned, but I knew it was totally humorous.

"Wait, go back." Blake handed Kyle his letter. "So you got in. Do Mom and Dad know?"

"Nah, not yet. I just got the mail a minute ago."

"So call them."

"I will, I will. First introduce me to your friends. Drama boy." Kyle looked at Charley. "You were in *The Diviners*, I remember. But who are these lovely ladies?"

"That's Marissa," I said, pointing. Marissa was absorbed in a paperback of *Romeo and Juliet*, holding a purple highlighter. "And I'm Skylar."

"No kidding? So you're the mutant."

"Excuse you?" My eyes opened so wide that I felt some of my mascaraed outer eyelashes unstick themselves from each other.

"The freshman chick in honors pre-calc. One of the lacrosse guys said there was a mad-smart freshman girl in his class."

"Yeah, that's me, then, the mutant."

What was I supposed to say? Here was a gorgeous guy, a senior, a soon-to-be Yalie for that matter, teasing me. I had to go along with it. Actually, for the rest of that year, I went along with whatever Kyle wanted. You would have too, if you had seen his blue eyes.

Right before first-semester finals, when I was

studying in the school library for my Spanish exam, Kyle came up behind me.

"Hey, mutant."

"Hey, Yalie. What's up?"

"Aw, nothing. My finals can go to hell. Unconditional acceptance to Yale, remember?"

"Wow, really? I'm so shocked! I didn't know about this before." I faked surprise.

"I'll help you. You've never taken a final before, right?"

"Yes, I have. I had to take math at the high school when I was in the seventh and eighth grades."

"Okay, big shot, then you don't want any help?"

"I'll take whatever you're giving."

"Well, in that case . . ."

At first I didn't know whether Kyle liked me or not. He was so much older than me, and I didn't have experience with seventeen-year-olds. Half the time I was trying to figure out how his mind worked, rather than comprehend what he was saying.

During spring semester, he always wanted to help me with my homework, though I never needed help. Multitasking through the work, we discussed literature, film, and politics. One day, we were sitting in the school library and he asked me to look at a parametric equation on his graphing calculator. Spelled out on the LCD screen was "Will you be my date to the dance?"

I melted. It was the nerdiest thing, getting asked out on a calculator screen, but that was Kyle. Creative and unusual and intriguing. I said yes, of course.

When I asked Blake if he would mind if I went to the Gala with his brother, he just shrugged. "Why not? I guess Kyle's still too freaked out from breaking up with that Michelle chick last semester to find an actual date."

But it *was* an actual date. It was the formal pre-graduation dance, the Graduation Gala, a sort of prom that went down two days after the seniors finished their finals, where the valedictorian and salutatorian were announced instead of king and queen. Kyle was salutatorian.

We were supposed to dance together after he got his award, but I was so self-conscious. There were all these seniors and I was barely fifteen, in a slinky black Donna Karan dress with my push-up bra squeezing my (minimal) boobs together so tight that they looked like a baby's ass strapped to my chest. I didn't want the seniors to stare at me and wonder why I was there.

But Kyle bent down in an elaborate bow, raising one eyebrow playfully. "Milady Mutant?"

I laughed, suddenly seeing Kyle and only Kyle, and danced with him slowly, my high heels lifting just an inch off the floor so I could rest my head on his neck and smell his cologne.

After the dance, Kyle took me back to his dorm room and closed the door, which he wasn't supposed to do, but I didn't say anything because he was a senior and I didn't want to be weird. He turned on his stereo, and Oasis crooned their beautiful lyrics, and we sat on his bed together, tired, and kicked off our shoes.

One of the slow songs on the album came on, and Kyle put his arm around my shoulder.

"Do you know how incredible you are?" he asked.

"Am I supposed to answer that?"

He laughed, squeezing my shoulder.

"Come on, Skylar. Be serious."

"I am serious."

"So am I. Seriously into you."

He leaned over and kissed me. It felt so soft and electric at the same time. I melted in his arms, and he slid me into his lap, easing himself down on the bed.

He gently kissed my face and neck, breathing softly in my ear. I didn't know how to respond, but it wasn't wrong, just sweet.

But when Kyle reached to undo the halter strap on my dress, I gasped as the dress fell down to my hips, revealing the padded strapless push-up bra I'd bought on sale at Victoria's Secret that year, confident no one would see it. The bra was bright green.

"Mmm, my little Girl Scout," he whispered, kissing my shoulder.

He slid his fingers under my bra clasp and tickled my back gently. I lay there passively as he unhooked my bra, kissing my neck and making me shiver with his warm breath.

Suddenly he had unbuttoned his shirt and I knew he wanted me to take off his tie. So I reached out, arms trembling, and slid it out from beneath his rigidly starched collar. Kyle smiled, extending a hand to tuck a strand of hair behind my ear. He guided my head gently onto his pillow, and I saw the muscles of his back coil as he removed his shirt and unzipped his pants.

I could see his erection through his boxer shorts, and he grabbed my wrist and placed my hand on his crotch. I stared at him, wide-eyed, until he sighed.

"You're supposed to move your hand."

"I know. It's just . . . I've never . . ."

"It's called a hand job, Skylar. It's not even oral sex. It's a *massage*."

I hesitated. I knew it wasn't a big deal, using my hand. But hand jobs were like JV fooling around, and I didn't want to go varsity too fast.

"You know what I like about you, Skylar?" Kyle said softly, kissing my neck. "You're a thinker. That's what you're doing right now, and it's so sexy."

He was so close to me, blue eyes, muscles, soft curly hair. I couldn't resist. So I nodded demurely and gave him a soft kiss on the mouth, and then everything else he asked for.

We spent the next week together, the last week before his graduation. I didn't want to tell Blake because it seemed to be too late for that— like my telling about Kyle would be an afterthought, an act of pity. I had these silly little fluttering emotions where I thought I was in love, but part of me knew that love isn't made to last in a fifteen-year-old heart. I had three years left at Hilliard; Kyle was starting college halfway across Connecticut.

After the first night, we met in Kyle's room when he thought his roommate wasn't going to be there, and at the old boathouse if his roommate was in the room. Kyle's roommate was Eric Gilmore, who was going to Brown even though he got B's, because he was a legacy. On the absolute last day seniors were on campus, Kyle and I were fooling around in his room when Eric walked in on us.

At first, I didn't realize that I was screwed— socially, I mean. I shrieked and grabbed for a blanket. I was embarrassed, but I thought that was going to be the end of it. Eric would laugh it off and the next day no one would know about it. But that's not what happened.

Eric was all, "Shit, man! Congrats."

Kyle gritted his teeth and asked, "Dude, do you think we could have a little privacy in here?"

Eric laughed, but then he got a look at me.

"Is that—nah, man! It can't be. Kyle, you're banging the freshman chick from pre-calc?"

"We weren't having sex," I piped up. God, what did Eric take me for? We were just, well, having varsity tryouts.

"Eric," Kyle warned, his voice going deep.

"Yeah, man. I'm out. Later." Eric shut the door, and I could hear his heavy footsteps in the hall.

"He's not going to . . ." I couldn't finish the sentence, because as I said it, I heard boys laughing loudly out in the hallway.

"I'm sorry, Skylar," Kyle said, rubbing my shoulder blades.

I shrugged him off and jammed my feet into my sparkly Chinatown slippers.

"This was a mistake," I told him.

"Sky, these things happen. It's no big deal. Everyone's leaving tomorrow."

"I'm not!" I practically screamed at him. "You keep forgetting that while you're going off to Yale, I'm going to be a lousy sophomore next year. And I'll be here the year after that, and the next year, too. God, Kyle, I'm never leaving this place. And now everyone's going to know and be talking about it—about me!"

"I really am sorry," Kyle offered.

"A googolplex of sorries can't fix this."

I couldn't swallow. My heart was stomping around in my rib cage and throwing a tantrum. My mouth didn't feel connected to my throat. My eyes were brimming with gray mascara. I wasn't going to cry. Good girls didn't cry over things like this, because good girls didn't do things like this.

Shamefully, in front of Kyle, I burst into tears. He stared at me, this appalled look on his face, probably wondering what had happened to the sultry sex goddess he'd been fooling around with five minutes ago. Because suddenly the sex kitten had become a plain old kitten, a sobbing, mewling baby. Kyle just stood there. He didn't pat me on the back or say it was okay, even though it wasn't. I could hear the boys in the hall hooting, and then one of them pounded on the door.

I had to get out of there. I buttoned my shirt and grabbed my tote bag.

"Wait." Kyle said the word carefully, as though he was just figuring out what I was doing. "You're leaving?"

"Yes. Goodbye."

I opened the door and was greeted by a parabola of smirking boys. Brushing the tears off my face, I marched down the hallway with as much dignity as I could glean from my shrinking ego.

"Skylar!" Kyle called, and I could have killed him for that. For giving the boys a name to go with the story. "Skylar! I'm sorry! Come back!"

I never turned around. I didn't need to see him one last time. Or ever again. He'd turned me into a slut while I was still a crying ninth grader. I needed to grow up.

When I got back to my room, I flopped onto my bed and cried until I was just forcing it. You'd think a girl like me wouldn't care what other people think, but I did. Any hope I had of being seen as a smart girl again, as a competitor for anything except other girls' boyfriends, was over. I would always be that girl who got caught. That story girls would use when guys tried to convince them to break visitation rules or close the door. And it embarrassed me no end. I knew I wasn't going to be expelled. No one was going to tell the head-master about Kyle and me.

By the time Marissa got back to the room from her anime club meeting, I'd composed myself and done a Mary Magdalene self-makeover as punish-ment. My eyeliner was thick and smoky. My nails were cherry-popping bloodred. I was wearing my one pair of high heels with my uniform khaki-pleated skirt. I was reading P. J. O'Rourke and smoking a borrowed cigarette from Anelise van der Drotten down the hall.

"I heard what happened," Marissa said, and then she got a good look at me and her jaw dropped. "Wow."

"Skip the palindromic interjections, please," I said, flipping a page in the aptly titled *Parliament of Whores*.

"Skylar . . . ," Marissa started to say, then trailed off. "I just thought . . . Are you okay?"

"No," I said. My throat felt funny from the crying and the cigarette, and my voice didn't sound like my own. "How in the world could I be okay? I'm officially the story of the year. The freshman in pre-calc, the copy editor of the school paper, the smart good girl caught in the act during finals with her friend's older brother." I sniffed, even though I wasn't crying. "God, Blake must despise me."

"Blake doesn't know," Marissa blurted.

I stared at her. How could he *not* know? It had been over an hour. Everybody knew.

"He's in the nurse's office with a migraine," she said. "He's staying all night—the nurse told me. Then we have the lit final tomorrow and we leave. No one will say anything to him with halls full of parents loading luggage into their SUVs. I talked to Charley, and he promised not to say anything, either. We'll make sure he never finds out. Situation under control."

Marissa was such a good friend. I exhaled some of the gross cigarette smoke, tottered over to her on my heels, and threw my arms around her.

"I'm disgusting," I said. "I deserve this misery."

"No you're not. And you don't. You and Kyle like each other, and you're so perfect together. It was kind of romantic, like in that book you just loaned me."

"Oh, Marissa, I'm so embarrassed. I should just switch back to Hackley or Loomis Chaffee or Taft or someplace for next year, but people will find out anyway. Everyone talks to everyone over the breaks."

When I got back to school the next year, the only person who didn't know was Blake. He had disappeared, moved back west to live with his parents, and I was left with a big scarlet letter appliquéd to my reputation.

That fall, according to the Hilliard School population, I was just a slut who had hooked up with half the seniors on the lacrosse team and been caught "servicing the equipment" and because I'd been caught on campus, the scandal wasn't quick to pass. It became a joke: "Don't get caught going down . . . the stairs!" It was awful, thank God I had a single room so I could study all day and then cry myself to sleep. I was miserable.

When Janice Weiner became slut of the year after spring break of my junior year, I felt horrible for her at first. But then I noticed how no one was whispering about me when I walked by anymore. I couldn't believe it was finally over. For a glorious two months, I was invisible, under the radar, and old news. There was just one year left until I could go to MIT, where practically no one from my school went.

Then I became senior honoree, and now some of the old attention has started up again when I pass people on the way to the dining hall or chapel or even the floor bathroom. Like I don't know what the Kims say about me behind my back, either. But this is a different type of whispering. This isn't "Oh, look at the trollop, isn't she a riot?" This is "Do you think she's the one who ruined the curve in Spanish last semester?"

And the scary thing? I kind of like it. For as long as I can remember, when I stood out here at Hilliard, it wasn't for something positive. At first I was appalled by my class rank, but I think that, gradually, I'll be okay with it. I'm starting to come to terms with the fact that I'm too extroverted to keep hiding, and besides, I enjoyed earning those

A's. I liked reading those articles about the kids who cracked the new SAT and got a 2400 because I'm part of that group. And as much as I pretend not to try so hard for any of these things, I realize that I still want them, and that I want to keep on trying. I don't want to sit down at graduation with my peers, just another kid wearing the same cap and gown as everyone else. I want to give the last speech of my high school career up on the podium. And I want the only photo people remember of me to be the class picture, me in the shawl and matching stiletto heels.

I read over what I had written and paused. I'd let myself become carried away by the story, by the need to finally get all this out and onto paper, like it was just another scandal I'd read somewhere, like it had happened to someone else. But what was I thinking? I couldn't turn this in. Not even if Mr. McCabe was the coolest teacher in the world. There was no way I could show this to him—to anybody. Time to write the "Why I Love Policy Debate" essay.

8

Charley: 100 Beers of Solitude

At first I just thought Blake had gotten up early and gone to smoke before class, but when he missed lunch, I figured okay, maybe something was going on. I didn't want to freak out Skylar and Marissa, though, so I didn't say anything about it.

The whole meal was weird. Skylar kept staring at me with one eyebrow raised as though she was thinking about having slept with me. Well, not *slept* slept with me. Crashed.

"What?" she said, because I was being quiet and thinking about the night before and where the hell Blake was.

"Nothing. I'm just tired," I said, and reached into my bag for a paperback: *100 Years of Solitude*. I changed books like I changed radio stations.

I read a page or two, drained my water glass, yawned, and told the girls goodbye. I was going to catch up on my sleep during the free period after lunch. As I was walking back to the dorm, my cell rang.

Caller ID blinked at me. Dad.

I flipped open the phone—top of the line, like every other gadget my dad bought after consulting everyone at his firm as well as *Consumer Reports*. His obsession with everything being the best even extended to consumer electronics.

"Hi," I said.

"What are you up to, son?"

I *hated* when he called me that. What did he think we were, the father, the son, and the holy Harvard?

"Not much, Dad."

Wait, that sounded like I was screwing around. Quickly, I added, "I mean, I'm studying so hard I don't have much free time."

There, that sounded better.

"Glad to hear it. Grades still high, Charley?"

"It's just summer session."

"That's not an answer."

Correction: it was an answer, just not an answer he wanted to hear. I clenched my fist.

"A's. I wrote a good essay for creative writing on when I started playing the guitar."

"That doesn't sound like a very challenging topic."

"It was the assignment." I stabbed the grass with the toe of my sneaker.

"Okay, then. Just checking. If I wasn't on top of you like this, you'd slack off."

"No I wouldn't."

"Don't argue with me, Charley. I know how things are at Hilliard. I went there, too."

Like I could forget. I sighed and waited for him to continue his cross-examination.

"How's Latin?"

"German, Dad. I'm in German now."

"Right."

He coughed, flustered.

"But you're not forgetting that Latin?"

"Got it covered. How's Ben?"

"He's taking up golf. Why don't you call him sometime? You're his big brother, Charley."

"I will. I know. But golf? Jeez, Dad, whose idea was that?"

"Your mother's. It's a fine sport. Many business deals are done on the green."

"It's not easy being green," I joked. Neither of us laughed.

"Listen, son, I have to see a client now, but I just wanted to touch base with you and make sure you were doing all right and enjoying your summer."

"I am. Everything's great."

"Glad to hear it. Take care, and get those SATs in shape, you hear?"

"Sure. Bye."

I slapped the phone closed and took my glasses off so I could pinch the bridge of my nose and try to de-stress. When I was on the second-floor stairs in Milbank, I gave the Class of '68 the finger.

Take that, Dad. Asshole-in-one.

"Blake?" I called, opening the door to our room. "I ganked a couple of cookies from lunch if you're hungry."

But he wasn't there.

Something was definitely wrong. I opened his closet. One of his duffel bags was gone. His drawers? A couple pairs of boxers, his uniform polos, not much else. His Dopp kit wasn't on his desk anymore, and neither was his cell phone.

"Shit!" I swore, kicking at his trash can. Blake had taken off.

I bent down to pick up the trash can, and knocked into the desk, stirring the computer out of sleep mode. We'd been having problems with the wireless in the dorm lately, where sometimes the connection would fall through mid–blog post or in the middle of sending an online form. I was obsessive about control-C copying everything before I sent it, and maybe Blake was, too. I opened a Word doc on his Mac and hit apple V, the paste command. A document pasted itself on the page, in a too big and misaligned font, which meant it was an e-mail. And as I started to read it, I knew what had happened.

Dear Kyle,

I'm sorry for being such an asshole little brother. You don't need to e-mail me anymore or anything because you clearly have your own life and I'm not part of it. I'm not even worthy to hear about it, I guess, since I was the only ignorant idiot at Hilliard who didn't know about you and Skylar. Mom and Dad are so happy you got into Yale that they can't imagine anything less from me, but goddamn it, I'm going to disappoint them. I'm going to disappoint everybody again. Something in me can't breathe in boarding school, and I thought it was Hilliard but it wasn't. It was me. I was the same screw-up in Corona Del Mar, and now I've gone and made a mess of everything again at Hilliard not even two damn weeks into summer session. I bet they'll kick me out, too.

I was so convinced that I could come back and everything would be the same with Skylar, Charley, and Marissa, just like freshman year, but I didn't even know what freshman year was about until now. I can't believe you. You pretended you went to that dance as "just friends," you asshole. You knew I liked her.

I thought this summer I'd have my chance with Skylar, but I was wrong. I was wrong about everything. No one told me anything back then, and they're still lying to me now.

I woke up and saw them together this morning, Skylar sleeping in bed with Charley, and Marissa keeping watch in a chair. I knew Skylar had been the one who saved my ass last night, which was so messed up because it was her fault in the first place, mostly, but it was all of their fault—yours, too. No one feels the way I do, they can't. Did they watch their brother and their roommate get with the girl they wanted, watch their dad sell off the summer homes and tell Mom to shop at Wal-Mart instead of Gelson's to save money? Did they have to pretend everything was the same when it wasn't, or get caught drinking vodka and get kicked out of their private day school? Don't try to understand me, Kyle. Just do your thing at Yale and make our parents proud enough for the both of us because I'm fucking finished. I'm gone. I'm a footnote in everyone else's life that's just gonna be skimmed over anyway. So I give up. I'm done with Hilliard before they can be done with me first. I only wish I hadn't come back and found out how unnecessary I was. Everyone's messed up and invisible in New York City, and no one cares. I'll fit right in, flow from party to party, just another rich kid on permanent vacation, just another stoner in the Sheep Meadow.

I must've stared at this page for fifteen minutes, reading it over until I understood, or thought I understood, what was going on. Blake had found out. At the party. Probably from those girls he was talking to.

Well, if that was the case, it was my fault. I had brought up Skylar's name, asking those girls if they'd seen her. Maybe if

I'd played it off, asked if they'd seen Pete Donahue next, gone through all the members of the debate team until she was just part of a list. I could have stayed with them, made sure they didn't talk about it. And made sure Blake didn't drink too much. Those girls were bad news from the moment they mentioned Kyle, but I was so disoriented by the party scene that I screwed up big-time.

Or, oh God, what if Blake had woken up when Skylar and I were talking? What if he'd heard it from us? I should have refused to let Skylar and Marissa stay the night, and dealt with Blake myself. He was my roommate, my responsibility, not theirs. I hadn't stopped him from going to that party. I hadn't stopped our conversation.

My fault my fault my fault.

At least he hadn't killed himself. He'd just run away.

Suddenly I wished J. D. Salinger had written some sort of sequel to *The Catcher in the Rye*, where Stradlater and Ackley and the rest of the kids at Holden's boarding school got to talk. Everyone at Hilliard was so into Salinger in ninth grade, toting around those little white paperbacks, using the word *phony* in their IMs and MySpace profiles. I never told anyone, but I thought the book had the wrong narrator. I wanted to hear from Holden's roommate, to read about his reaction when Holden disappeared from the dorm that night. Did he go after Holden, chase him around Manhattan like a detective, or just let him disappear?

One thing was for certain: I couldn't let Blake disappear. He was a good roommate, a friend, a decent guy, even if he was the main source of trouble in my life. But what could I do?

I was stuck at summer session, and it wasn't exactly like my parents would understand if I got up and left. Not like my parents understood anything else I wanted to do.

I printed out Blake's e-mail and got out my guitar so I could think. I turned the volume on my amp up a decent amount, not caring if anyone was trying to study or sleep. I played some old Clapton, singing along softly, until my mind slowly became unglued from the chord changes and the strum pattern, and I was in that place between the pickups where there was space just enough to think.

I thought about what Skylar and I had talked about last night, and I tried to picture myself at Harvard, going to organic chemisty and biology recitations and labs. I tried to picture myself cutting open a cadaver, wearing a white lab coat—or was that med school? All I knew was that when I thought about college, I thought about acting, and music, and cool professors like Mr. McCabe.

I wasn't going to be a doctor, I realized. It was never going to happen, because it wasn't me. It was my parents. And for a moment, I envied Blake, because even though he was a screw-up, at least he was in control of his own goddamn life. He was the master of his fate, the captain of his soul. And I was the one following a road map.

I was seventeen, and it was about time I did something big. Huge. Like go after Blake.

No, maybe not that. I couldn't. It would be Ivy League suicide. Plus, it would guarantee that Skylar became the valedictorian. Unless she came with me.

What if we all did it? All three of us. We could probably

find him. How many parties could there be in the Manhattan private school network? Didn't everybody know everybody?

No, that was insane. We couldn't just leave.

I lay back on my bed, reading over Blake's e-mail again. First I had to tell Skylar and Marissa about what had happened. It was my responsibility, because I'd found the e-mail. Maybe we could discover a lead, some clue where he'd run off to, what his actual plans were.

I groaned. *Goddamn it, Blake!* This was not what I'd had in mind when I signed up for summer session to get away from my parents.

9

Skylar: Get Lost in a Good Bookmark

Charley and Marissa and I never had a society of sworn secrecy regarding oral sex with salutatorians. There wasn't any elaborate moonlit ceremony in hooded robes and Grecian sandals. It was a simple pact, an understanding that each of us would do our part to make sure Blake never found out.

I didn't blame Charley. How could I? When he told me what had happened, he turned as white as Blake's "spearmint Tic Tacs," and kept rubbing his glasses on the hem of his shirt.

"Look," Charley said, fiddling with his lenses, "it's about Blake."

The three of us were sitting at one of the crappy ends of the dining hall tables, near the trash can. We were eating pot roast, which everyone called "marijuana meat," just to be funny.

Charley stuttered, "Last night, um, Blake found out about the—the thing."

"The thing?" Marissa asked.

"Well, if you want to be specific, *Kyle's* thing," he said.

"Oh. Wow." Marissa speared a string bean with her fork.

I stared intensely at the string bean, realizing that we'd been talking about Kyle last night. Damn it.

"It gets worse," Charley said. "I found this e-mail he sent to his brother about it. He was really pissed. And he took off."

"What do you mean, took off?" I asked.

"He's in New York, partying."

"Shit," I said solemnly. "Is he coming back?"

"He isn't picking up his phone, and he took his stuff with him, so I'd say it wasn't just a day trip."

"Do you still have the e-mail?" Marissa asked.

"Yeah." Charley handed each of us a stapled document.

I read the e-mail. Wow. Blake *was* pissed. And Marissa had been right all along, Blake *had* liked me.

"This isn't good," I said, putting down my copy of the e-mail. My heart was racing.

"I'm sorry," Charley said. "It's my fault. He found out either at that party, from those Kim chicks I left him with, or because I didn't realize that he was awake when we were talking. If I'd been careful, maybe . . ."

"Oh shut up, Charley," I told him softly, patting his arm. "It's not your fault. Or any of our faults. Yeah, maybe he wouldn't have found out last night, but we can't watch him all the time. Sooner or later it had to happen. There's no reason to freak out because it may or may not have been us who told him."

After trying to console Charley, I felt a little bit better, but then I thought about it and realized that I actually felt a lot worse. Blake was gone. As in he'd run away from Hilliard. No one did that. It wasn't done. Just like no one bragged about having a first-class plane ticket home for the holidays, and no one wore Princeton sweatshirts after April if they were rejected, people didn't just take off. But Blake had, and he'd done it because of me.

I ate some more of my marijuana meat and thought about the situation. Charley and Marissa stared at me.

"I was wondering," Marissa said. "You didn't keep in touch with Kyle, did you?"

"Of course not," I said quickly, even though I hadn't deleted the number from my phone. I never deleted numbers. How else could I screen my incoming calls?

"Well, that sucks," Marissa told me. "The easiest way to figure out where Blake is would be to call his brother."

I shook my head. No way was that happening.

"Let's try to reason through this," Charley said, and I could literally picture a Venn diagram floating around in his head. "What do we know about Blake?"

"He's in New York," Marissa said.

"He was popping pills," I said. Marissa and Charley stared at me like I'd just told them I wanted to get a summer job at Dress Barn so I could use the employee discount.

"What?" Marissa said.

"Pills. He had bottles of them in his messenger bag, and he used to stick them in Tic Tac containers, but how obvious is it when he swallows the 'Tic Tac' whole?"

"What do you think he was taking?" Marissa asked.

"It looked like prescription stuff. You know, the crap that people deal to each other out of their parents' medicine cabinets. Tylenol with codeine, Ritalin, Adderall, Xanax, Klonopin."

"Jesus." Charley ran his hand through his hair. "He was more messed up than I thought. It must have been because of his family."

His family. Oh my God, that was right—the e-mail had said how they'd lost their money.

"It's just so surreal," I said. "I can't picture Blake poor."

"Poor by *your* standards, maybe," Marissa said, rolling her eyes. "But I'm sure it wasn't *that* bad."

"No one likes to lose something," I reminded her, "especially not something they take for granted, like their parents' money."

Charley cleared his throat and rustled his copy of Blake's e-mail. I totally knew how he felt. My parents had always taught me not to talk about money, too. It was a dirty subject, like discussing which parts of your body you had shaved during your morning shower.

"Should we tell the school?" Marissa asked.

"I don't think so," Charley said. "They wouldn't understand. Blake's not usually like this. He's just going through some rough shit, you know? But they wouldn't see it that way. They'd treat him like some criminal."

"Charley's right," I said. "He could be expelled. It would completely screw up his future. What if the school found him with the drugs and turned him over to the police? Arrested under the influence and in the possession of pot and/or illegally obtained prescription medicine."

We were all quiet after that. While Marissa and Charley dug into their dinners, I made a mental list of reasons the three of us were obligated to do something about Blake:

1. We were the only ones who knew he had left. Except Kyle, but I wasn't going there. We could deal with this on our own.
2. We were one of the reasons he left. Okay, technically *I* was one of the reasons Blake left, but in his e-mail he was bitching about how I was Charley's girlfriend, which I'm not, so Blake actually left because he thought I was dating *Charley*. So it was both of us.
3. We were his friends. Even though Blake could be kind of a pompous jerk, he was still part of our original four, part of the two sets of roommates. Friends didn't desert friends, especially since we were the cause of his misery (for misery, see #2).

I went over my list while I ate my "baked" (aka dubiously microwaved) potato.

"When do we leave?" I asked Charley and Marissa.

They stared at me.

"Admit it—you guys were thinking about it, too."

"I *was* thinking about it, yeah," Charley admitted. "I think he needs us. I don't know if there's anyone else."

"Good, then it's set," I told him.

"No, it's not," Marissa said. "We're going up to Charley's

room right now to see if Blake left any hints. The name of a hotel, the address of a party. I'm not running away to New York without a plan."

"Don't worry," I said. "Neither are we."

This was how I found myself trying to hack into Blake's laptop with Charley and Marissa hanging over my shoulders.

I opened the Safari Internet browser and typed "a" into the Web address box, waiting for the computer to "remember" the rest of the address. Nothing. I tried B. Then C. Nothing.

"What about e-mail accounts?" Marissa asked. "He wouldn't use a school account to send that."

I tried Gmail, Yahoo, and Hotmail. None of them had been signed into.

"Bookmarks?" Charley asked, and I checked the bookmarks. CNN, Amazon, Google.

"This is useless," I said, clicking on a familiar MSN messenger icon and trying to sign in with Blake's ID—teenage-mutantganjaturtle17. Enter a password. Yeah, not happening.

"It's like he doesn't even use that Internet browser," Marissa said.

"Whoa," Charley said. "You're right. Here, let me see that for a minute."

Charley leaned over my shoulder and ran the mouse over each icon at the bottom of the screen so the names displayed.

"Firefox," he muttered, opening a different Internet browser.

Charley clicked on "bookmarks," and suddenly we had a list of, uh, teenage boy Web sites.

"Oh," I said uncomfortably as Charley scrolled through the names.

"Wait," he said, clicking on one called cutiexsaraxsauce's Livejournal.

It was some girl's too pink blog filled with online "At your 10-year high school reunion" and "Which O.C. character are you?" quizzes.

Then there was a short blog entry dated last week: "im so drunk haha great party at some columbia dorm woah . . . got to get blake to come to one of these some time hed love this shit. yeah im going to bed now. later losers and come out next thursday to joshs suite lots of jd so i might show late."

We all looked at each other after reading this. Our first lead. Blake would probably see this friend in New York and go to Josh's dorm party with her. They'd show up late.

It was something.

"Click back on the bookmarks," I said, and there it was, right beneath cutiexsaraxsauce's blog. A bookmark for Columbia University's campus map.

10

Charley: It Is a Far, Far Crazier Thing I Do than I Have Ever Done Before

On the night before Skylar and Marissa and I left for New York, after I'd found Blake's e-mail, Pete "Sticks" Donahue and I were in the dorm kitchen making Hilliard s'mores. Here's how to do it: Get graham crackers, Hershey bars, and marshmallows, make a sandwich, stick it in the microwave, and hope it melts before it explodes.

We could just as easily have toasted the marshmallows on the stove burner, but I didn't think of that, and besides, it would have taken away from the microwaved glory that is the Hilliard s'more.

I was hanging out with Pete because my room felt empty without Blake, plus Skylar had made me promise that we wouldn't hang out together until we went after Blake, so everyone wouldn't see the three of us and realize Blake was missing.

Pete was okay. He'd gotten his nickname as a freshman, when Ashton Hadley told Pete he was so skinny that his arms and legs looked like sticks. But even though I got along with Sticks, he still wasn't Blake. *He* didn't try to open the door of the microwave exactly a nanosecond before the timer beeped.

"Dude, your roommate should join debate this year," Sticks told me through a mouthful of s'more.

"Yeah?" I asked.

"Yeah. He's in my philosophy and Moral Issues section. Jesus. You should hear what he talks about. He's just about got the class convinced that he's the Antichrist. A natural Lincoln-Douglas Debate type. I'd sign him up for the team in a second. Could you imagine how he'd slaughter in novice?"

"It would be wicked funny to watch," I admitted.

Suddenly a bunch of freshman guys ran past the kitchen screaming at the top of their lungs. One of the boys was clutching a towel around his skinny ass and running after a kid who was carrying a pair of flip-flops.

"Give me my goddamn shower shoes, Gabe!" the kid in the towel yelled, and Gabe and his friends laughed.

They ran up and down the hall, then jumped onto the crappy lounge furniture and ping-pong table. There were four of them, all acne-smeared. I leaned my head out of the kitchen and watched to see how it ended.

"Break it up, come on, guys," someone called from the stairs, and I craned my neck to see around the vending machines.

It was Mr. McCabe.

"Let's go. I mean it," McCabe said, stepping into the lounge and staring them down at close range.

The freshmen disengaged, and Gabe gave Towel Boy back his shower shoes.

Mr. McCabe sighed and said, "Oh, hey, Charley."

"Hi, Mr. McCabe. What are you doing in the dorm?"

"Consider me Milbank's stepparent," he said. "Bloom needed the night off."

Mr. Bloom, the AP bio teacher, was our regular dorm parent. He smelled like cottage cheese and tuna fish and wore the same corduroy pants all week long.

"Did he have a hot date?" I joked.

"No, he went to a rave," Mr. McCabe returned.

I smiled, because most teachers didn't know what a rave was, and they definitely wouldn't joke about it. I'd get an A in his class for sure.

"Charley, is your roommate around? I need a word with him."

Crap. How could I explain that Blake was probably sleeping in some girls dorm room at Columbia?

"Uhhh, actually, I haven't seen him."

"You're sure? Because he missed class today and didn't turn in the last assignment."

"Really? I'll ask him about that when I see him."

"Great. Thanks, Charley, I appreciate it. Why don't you walk with me? I'm heading back downstairs."

"Sure thing."

I turned to Pete, who shrugged. He had chocolate smeared all around his mouth.

"Later, Sticks," I said, attempting to clean up quickly by throwing my paper towel and a candy wrapper into the trash can.

"Lead the way, O Captain, my Captain," I said to Mr. McCabe.

"Ah, the auspicious poetic stylings of Mr. Whitman," McCabe said, walking down the stairs as I followed.

Just like always, I stopped right before the bottom step and stared at my dad's year, sixty-eight. He'd gone by "Chuck" back in his boarding-school days. Chuck Morton Jr. I smiled, because Dad was going to hate me for what Skylar and Marissa and I were going to do, going after Blake. Dad was big on survival of the fittest in boarding school; he'd had a single for most of his sophomore year after he turned in his roommate to the dorm parent for smoking grass in the room. Bastard.

"Something caught your eye?" McCabe asked.

"Nothing," I said, looking away from the solemn stare my dad had shot the camera all those years ago.

McCabe came up next to me on the step and stared at the portrait.

"Which one's your father?" he asked me.

"How did you know?"

"Just guessing. Which is he?"

"In the shawl."

McCabe nodded.

"Must be hard, having to live up to his expectations."

I stared at him in surprise.

"Yeah, but I'm used to it."

"I want to show you something," Mr. McCabe said.

We walked halfway up the stairs.

"What are we looking for?" I asked.

"This." Mr. McCabe motioned toward a class picture.

"Which one was you?"

He pointed. The picture looked like it could have been taken yesterday, even though the date on the bottom was seven years ago. McCabe was in the front row, grinning, with his arms thrown over the shoulders of two guys. His hair was a little longer in the picture, but other than that, nothing had changed. I scanned the names at the bottom of the picture to see who his friends were. Theodore Marcus Dalton, Yale. Ethan Bell McCabe, Brown. Nathaniel John Kent-Stockton, Duke.

Wait.

"Bell?" I asked. "As in Headmaster Bell?"

McCabe smiled.

"As in Headmaster Grandpa. Like I said, must be hard, having to live up to your dad's expectations."

"Wow. Does it get easier?"

"It depends. It's never easy, Charley, to tell people who love you that you want to be someone different than who they want you to be."

"Who did you want to be?"

"A writer. But don't you dare say 'Those who can't do, teach,' or I'll fail your sorry ass," McCabe joked.

"Never."

We walked back down the stairs.

"I have to admit," he told me, "I was hoping I'd run into you tonight."

This guy was a riot. Next he was going to say that he wanted to invite me to join a secret literary society that met by the old boathouse and recited haiku or something.

"What do you mean?"

"I'd like to talk to you and your friends about Blake," Mr. McCabe said, and I had an "oh shit" moment.

"The corner room," I said, trying not to freak out.

McCabe knocked, and Skylar opened the door in jeans and a gloriously low-cut pink tank top. I still couldn't believe she had slept over the night before. It seemed unreal.

"What's going on?" she asked suspiciously, staring at Mr. McCabe.

"Can we come in? Mr. McCabe wants to talk with us about Blake," I said.

Skylar shrugged and plopped down on her bed. I sat next to her. Marissa was at her desk, so Mr. McCabe took Skylar's desk chair.

"Look," Mr. McCabe said, "is Blake having any problems? Maybe with his family, or with a girlfriend? He hasn't been doing his work, and he didn't show up to class today. You're his friends, and I'd like to know what's happening here."

"Nothing," Marissa said. "We haven't seen Blake, either."

"Interesting choice of words, Ms. Rodolf," McCabe said. "You might not have *seen* Blake, but you know something, don't you?"

Marissa shrugged and examined a strand of her hair.

"How about you, Mr. Morton? Anything?"

"Nope," I said simply.

"Nice essay, by the way." He grinned at me, and suddenly Mr. McCabe didn't seem like a teacher so much as a cool older-brother type. "Stop by my office sometime and we can talk guitar."

"You play?" I asked incredulously.

"White Fender Stratocaster, just like Hendrix." He nodded.

"Cool. Got any Hendrix tabs?"

"You'll just have to stop by and see."

I was tempted. But what if he was just acting all buddy-buddy with us so we'd confess what had happened to Blake? Then we'd get slammed with the responsibility for it and go up against the Honor Board. Not like Pete Donahue, Eunice Kim, Ali Ahmad, and the rest of them had anything on us. But still. No way was I going to say anything. I hoped Skylar would do the same.

"Mr. McCabe?" Skylar asked.

This was it. Skylar was going to rat. I shut my eyes, waiting for it.

"Maybe you should check with the nurse or something. I know he gets migraines sometimes."

I opened my eyes, breathing a sigh of relief.

Mr. McCabe sighed.

"Okay. Fine. If you have anything to tell me later on, though, I'd really appreciate it."

Before we could swear that we had no idea what he was talking about, Mr. McCabe got up and walked toward the door.

"Have a good night. And leave the door propped while Charley's here. Otherwise I'll have to write you up for a dorm rule violation."

After McCabe left, I sat next to Skylar on her bed and tried to imagine what it would be like if my grandpa was the headmaster. Then I tried to think how long it had been since I'd taken an SAT practice test. I couldn't remember.

11

Skylar: Dress Your Family in Corduroy and Denigration

We met during lunch by the lake, not on the boathouse side, but where the canopy for the regatta was usually set up.

While I waited for Charley and Marissa to show up, I kept thinking about that day when Blake came back. I saw the fluttering white canopy, the trays of untouched Ex-Lax brownies, the look on Blake's face as I told him that things fell apart. I'd been talking about the past, but what I said had applied to the future as well. His future.

"Hey," Marissa said. "So where's Charley?"

"He better not be chickening out," I said, flipping my hair. "We're not going without him."

Two minutes went by. I stared at my watch and made little impatient noises. Finally Charley showed up.

"Good, you came," I said.

"What do you mean?" he asked.

"Oh, I dunno," I said. "I thought you'd flake on us,

Charley. You know, talk yourself out of it instead of declining nouns last period. I'm glad."

"Jeez," Charley said. "I just had to use the bathroom. It wasn't like I was planning on hanging around for turkey taco Thursday."

The way he said it, though, I knew he almost had. And he still looked hesitant, the way my mom had in Bloomie's right before she put back the Prada bag I wanted, saying it was too sophisticated for someone my age.

So I threw my arms around Charley and gave him a huge hug. My head was squeezed into his chest, the buttons on his oxford-cloth shirt pressing into my cheek. He smelled faintly like soap and belt leather and boy. Actually, he smelled like Kyle had, and my heart felt totally funny when I realized it.

Charley started hugging me back, which made me think how it was kind of weird that we were standing there practically all over each other, so I pulled away.

We crept down to the gates and hunched behind some bushes. After a couple of minutes, a Lexus pulled up to the gates and we snuck through while the driver argued with the security guard in the gatehouse.

Once we were through the gates, we made a break for the closest bus stop. As we ran, I felt my backpack bang into my spine with each step, and I whined and cursed the thing under my breath. Maybe I shouldn't have packed my blow-dryer, hair-straightening iron, and Kiehl's shower products?

"I've got it," Charley said, slipping my backpack off and slinging it over one of his shoulders.

"Thanks." I smiled gratefully.

"Oh, Charley, I don't think I'm going to make it. Could you carry my change of clothes and toothbrush, too?" Marissa teased.

"Yeah, yeah. We can't all be as strong as you," I told her.

"Because some of us are worried about chipping their nail polish?" Marissa smirked.

"Not even! This polish has been chipped for days. I have more important things to worry about than my cuticle beds."

"If your cuticles are so anxious to go to bed, maybe they should get a room," Marissa joked, cracking herself up.

When we made it to the bus stop, completely out of breath, Charley flung the backpacks on a bench and complained, "What do you have in there, your calc textbook?"

"Which is heavier," I demanded, "my calc book or your SAT prep books?"

Charley blushed, and I felt horrible for teasing him about that stuff. He couldn't help wanting to do well. None of us could. I'd photocopied my homework and stuck it in my bag. Obviously we have all those library print credits so we don't have to lug textbooks with us when we run away from school and plan on returning with our work done.

The bus pulled up, and the three of us climbed on and squished together onto one of the few vacant rows.

At the train station, Charley and Marissa and I sat in these hard plastic chairs near the departures board, waiting for it to show the platform number for the MetroNorth train into Grand Central.

Charley had his headphones on, iPod inside the pocket of

the Harvard hoodie he was wearing over his polo. Marissa was sketching anime people again in her little pink notebook, drawing them with perky boobs and knee-high boots.

"Add some buckles," I advised.

"What?"

"On their boots."

"But they're Sailor Scouts," Marissa protested.

I grabbed the pencil and made the boots look cooler, then added shrunken blazers with little elbow patches.

"Perfect." I handed her back the pencil, satisfied.

Marissa studied the picture.

"I like it," she said, adding velvet riding hats and crops. "Scouts in disguise. Very James Bond."

"You mean James Bondage," I said, and Marissa shrugged.

We lapsed into silence while Marissa sketched and Charley listened to his music.

Finally the departures board displayed the platform numbers for Boston and New York.

"Number three," Marissa said, standing up. "Come on."

Platform three was pretty shady. There was just the elevator (graffiti-splashed), the metal staircase (covered in gum wads), a rack of Christian Science literature (in my perfect world, the free magazine racks would all be crammed full of British *Vogue* and *Scientific American*), and a putrid orange overhang (enough said).

We made our way up the entire length of the platform to the very front cars, where practically nobody goes because they're lazy and don't want to walk. There were two girls, maybe thirteen, in one of the cars we looked into. They seemed okay, so we stepped inside and scored two bench seats facing each other. Perfect.

Marissa suddenly looked like she was about to pass out or something.

"Are you okay?" I asked.

"My parents are going to kill me," she whispered.

"Marissa, you've never done anything remotely wrong in your life. They won't kill you. They'll probably be thrilled that you're participating in a little old-fashioned teenage rebellion."

"No, they'll kill me," Marissa said. "They didn't even want me to go away to Hilliard, but I got a scholarship and they figured nothing bad ever happens in Connecticut. New York City is different."

I sighed, frustrated. She was getting cold feet *now*? We'd already bought the tickets. We were already on the train. We were—was that a lurch? Yup—already moving.

"Uh, Marissa?" I said gently.

"I know," she moaned. "I should have thought this through better."

"Actually, I was going to say that the train is already on its way to New York."

Marissa looked out the window; then she turned toward me, her eyes huge.

"It's really happening?" she asked.

"And don't you dare feel guilty," I said. "We're doing the right thing. So what if our parents yell? Are any of us even that close to our parents? We don't even live at home, so it's not like they'll miss us."

"I guess. But what about the DC?"

"No way they'd expel us," Charley added, headphones around his neck. "We're friends with half of the Disciplinary Committee anyway. Plus they've never expelled a legacy before. If I'm safe, then we're all safe. The way I see it, the blame is on Blake's ass or no one's."

Marissa sighed. Then the two girls I'd basically forgotten about started talking, so we shut up and eavesdropped.

"Did you hear about Carla?"

"No, what?"

"So you know how her boyfriend rows crew? Rumor is, she was caught with him out by the lake trying out for coxswain."

"Wait, I'm confused. I thought she was caught giving him a bl—"

"That's what I mean! God, Lauren found them. And then she texted me and wanted to know what to do. So I was like, tell the whole school. She deserves it. Skank."

"Yeah, she totally does. I should write about it in my blog, too. Slut." The girls laughed uproariously.

Whoa. This was so not happening to me. It was unbelievable. Out of all the cars on the train, I was stuck in one with these annoying tweens who had nothing better to do than perpetuate the kind of gossip I'd spent years trying to escape. Ugh. Disgusting.

Charley and Marissa were looking at me like I was going to burst into tears. Well, I wasn't. Sure, it sucked when things like this happened, when I saw girls being cruel, but I wasn't going to let it ruin my day. I tried to smile and shrug, like I wasn't bothered by any of it.

Marissa reached over and squeezed my hand, her anxiety attack forgotten.

"Whatev, I'm fine," I mumbled.

I leaned my head against the window and stared out at the sine wave of the trees as we sped past.

12

Charley: New York State of Mind Control

I couldn't believe there was actually someone somewhere who thought it would be a good idea to name a bread store Hot and Crusty and then proceed to place this store strategically inside Grand Central Station.

"Hot and Crusty," I said out loud. The store sounded like the symptoms of some rare STD.

Skylar laughed, playing with her hair as we walked through the crowded station. "Oh yes, that's exactly how I like my men."

"Well, I'd prefer warm and gooey," Marissa announced, then realized what she'd said and turned bright red.

We laughed our asses off at that one.

We walked up the sloping pathway toward the street level, opening the heavy doors and just soaking in the atmosphere of the city, the constant hum and glitter, the background noise of millions of people living within the same few square miles. The whole thing was even more of a rush because we were supposed to be having dinner with the rest of the summer-session kids back at Hilliard. I got to thinking I should have rebelled a long time ago.

When we walked outside, the heat pressed in on me until I was slightly dizzy.

There was a line of people so long that I thought they all had to be waiting for something spectacular, like free Ivy League diplomas. Then I saw one person at the front of the line duck into a taxi. As soon as the taxi took off, another one replaced it, like the first one had never been there at all.

That was how New York City seemed to me: full of impermanence.

"Omigod, it is so *hot*," Skylar squealed. "I'm melting."

She was right. Maybe all the skyscrapers and taxis and people jumbled together were keeping the heat locked between the buildings, because it was definitely getting more and more uncomfortable by the minute.

"Uh, Skylar?" I asked. "Have we decided on a place to stay?"

"Oh, Charley." She laughed. "I've totally got this covered. We're meeting my friend Cal at the SoHo Grand in half an hour."

Cal? Who the hell was this dude? And why was he allowing us to stay with him?

"What's the SoHo Grand?" Marissa asked.

"It's a hotel. In SoHo," Skylar said, rolling her eyes.

"I don't have enough money for a hotel room," Marissa said.

"You won't need it," Skylar said as we got in the taxi line.

Skylar slipped into our cab as though she had been doing it her entire life.

"West Broadway and Grand, please," she said as Marissa and I slid in after her.

It was hard to remember she'd grown up in New York. Well, maybe not the city.

"Where's Tarrytown again?" I asked.

"About an hour away," she said, and then, "God, I love it here."

"This *is* a nice cab," Marissa teased. "I'm starting to fall in love with it myself."

I didn't say anything. My window was cranked down and I'd stuck my head out so I could see the tops of buildings.

"Incredible," I mumbled, not caring that I sounded/looked/felt like a tourist. The buildings in Manhattan reminded me of computer chips glistening, and the sun was setting in a way that they all seemed to ripple in the shadows.

We pulled up near this expensive-looking hotel, the kind my parents usually dragged me to have tea at when we went on vacations together. I paid the cab fare, even though Skylar protested. I wanted to show her how much better I was than that Cal person, who I hoped was her cousin or something.

Marissa and I followed Skylar, something we'd been doing a hell of a lot of lately, through the lobby and into the crammed elevator. We got out a couple floors up and walked into this lounge.

I scanned the area quickly, looking for Blake, which was stupid because, really, what were the odds that we'd find him in half an hour? Instead, I found a gorgeous blonde. She was sipping something pink and her long hair covered more of her breasts than her top did. Wow.

Suddenly, the blonde looked right at me. Oh God. She was smiling. She got up. She was walking over! *Stay cool, Charley. Don't be a loser. You don't have a chance with her—you like Skylar. Remember Sky—*

"Skylar!" the blonde squealed. They hugged and said "Oh my God" loudly.

People stared, and I crammed my hands in my pockets and stared at my feet.

"Charley, Marissa, this is my friend Callie Minter. We went to Dalton together until I moved to Tarrytown in fourth grade."

"Nice to meet you." I stuck out my hand, because I thought I should. Minter. As in the family who owned half the magazines in New York? Damn. But then Callie laughed and swatted my hand away and gave me a hug.

She was gorgeous and had great breasts and smelled fantastic. But she wasn't Skylar. Still, I enjoyed it all the same.

"Aww," Callie cooed after she'd stopped hugging me, "Charley's blushing. Sky, he's so adorable."

Adorable? Hell yeah.

"John Mayer adorable or fuzzy puppy adorable?" I persisted, grinning.

"John Mayer holding a puppy adorable. Now check your ego at the concierge desk, Charley," Skylar deadpanned, rolling her eyes.

"How long are you guys going to need the suite for?" Callie asked.

"The suite?" Marissa asked.

"Well, yeah," Callie said. "Skylar said you needed to crash at the suite my parents keep here."

She handed each of us a room card. Score!

"A couple of nights," Skylar said. "Two, maybe three."

"Hey, listen, thanks a lot," I told Callie. "I really appreciate you letting us crash here."

"Why not?" Callie shrugged. "Everyone does. Half the seniors at Dalton have probably been drunk in that room sometime in the past year."

"I'll keep that in mind," I said dryly.

The four of us headed up to the room.

The suite was the size of an airplane hangar or the Hilliard gym—if they'd added a plasma TV, an oversized Jacuzzi, and a king-sized bed.

"Wow," Marissa said, giggling.

I tossed my backpack onto a chair and hurled myself at the bed.

"Argh!" I yelled, making a life-sized imprint on the down comforter as I moved my arms and legs, snow angel style.

Callie laughed, and I flipped over and stared at the girls.

"Plenty of room," I suggested.

Skylar slipped her feet out of her shoes and leapt on top of me.

"Umph. You're too heavy," I teased. "Go on a diet."

Of course Skylar, who was probably a size negative three-quarters or something, giggled and tried to smother me with one of those decorative satin pillows.

"Take that back," she demanded, dissolving into laughter.

"Hey, um," Marissa said, "are we going to eat soon?"

"You're hungry?" Callie asked her, then wrinkled her nose and said, "I am too."

"I'd *like* to eat something," Skylar said sarcastically, "but seeing as how I'm so *fat* and everything . . ."

"Oh, shut up, you know you're gorgeous," I said, then cleared my throat awkwardly. "Um, room service?"

I was excited at the prospect of a meal that hadn't come from the infectory—I mean refectory—at Hilliard. Blake always thought the nickname was hysterical and still used it, probably because he never got the memo that the school had started calling it the dining hall two years ago.

Callie picked up the room phone and asked us what we wanted.

Burgers. Fries. Cokes. Actually, that was three Cokes and something called a "Voss sparkling" for Callie.

After she hung up the phone, I asked her what she'd ordered.

"Oh, you don't know what Voss is? It's only the best water in the world. Imported from Norway and everything."

"Just so long as it isn't Armani, I'm sure it tastes super," I joked.

Callie pointed a finger at Skylar and said, "He is adorable! Where did you find him?"

"Craigslist, under 'casual encounters,' " Skylar teased.

"What's that?" Marissa asked. No one told her.

There was a knock at the door a few minutes later. Room service. Now, I've had some pretty good burgers in my life, but these were like patties of filet mignon.

After we ate the burgers and Callie made everyone take a

sip of her wholly unremarkable water ("Omigod, you have to try this. You'll never ever want to drink anything else ever again!") I took a pack of playing cards out of my backpack and shuffled.

"Ooh, strip poker!" Callie enthused.

"How about not," I said. I didn't need the pressure of trying to keep everything in the pants department under control if I was in a room with three topless teenage girls, two of whom had C cups (or so I surmised).

"Twenty-one questions?" Skylar asked.

"Omigod, I haven't played that with you in forever!" Callie squealed.

"It's this game we used to play," Skylar explained. "I think we invented it, but maybe it's just one of those things that everyone thinks only they know about. Anyway, it's played like blackjack, but the winner gets to ask a question and everyone else has to answer. We play twenty-one games of blackjack like that."

"What kind of questions?" Marissa asked suspiciously.

"Don't worry, sweetie," Callie said, "the game is only as embarrassing as you make it. Besides, it's not like we'll know if you make stuff up."

"You can always pass," Skylar said.

Marissa nodded. "I'm in. Charley can be the dealer."

When she said that, Skylar and I exchanged a look. Dealer. Blake. We needed to find him. What the hell were we doing playing some stupid card game with a designer-water-obsessed heiress when we could be at Columbia looking for Blake?

"Nothing happens this early," Skylar said, sensing what I was thinking. "We'll go out later."

"Okay."

I dealt. Clockwise from me were Marissa, Callie, and Skylar. Marissa won the first hand with twenty.

"Okay, um, where do you want to go to college?" she asked.

"Brown," Callie said.

Skylar said, "MIT," and waited expectantly for me to answer.

I thought about all the things she'd asked me the other night: what I would do if I could have any job in the world, why I was letting my parents run my life, if I even liked science and math enough to survive pre-med.

I said, "I don't know."

"Wait," Marissa said. "I thought you wanted to go to Harvard."

"No, my *dad* wants me to go to Harvard," I said. "Right now, I'm undecided."

Skylar smiled, and I dealt again. This time Callie hit twenty-one. She lit a cigarette in triumph.

"Okay, like, what's something you've never told anyone?" she asked, exhaling smoke through her nostrils. "And you better make it good."

Skylar sighed. "I hate you for that one," she told Callie.

"Oh, whatever. You know you love me. Now spill!" Callie chirped.

Skylar rolled her eyes and admitted, "I was a kindergarten dropout."

"What?" I asked, surprised.

"I am not telling you this." She shook her head, like she was disgusted with herself.

"Skylar," I said, putting my hand on her pants leg, "it's okay not to be perfect. Remember? Come on, now you've made me curious, so you have to tell us what happened."

"It's embarrassing."

"Uh, that's the point!" Callie said. "Besides, it's not like I don't already know. Now tell your boyfriend so we can all move on."

"He's not—oh, fine. When I was really little, my parents found me reading the newspaper they'd left on the coffee table. They got so excited that they started giving me all these books. Then they took me to this doctor so I could be tested. You know, for my IQ? He told them it might be a good idea to put me in school right away. I was only three! All the other kids made fun of me and it was so horrible that I pretended to be stupid so I wouldn't have to go to school anymore."

I'd always wondered why Skylar hadn't skipped a grade. I looked over at her, and she looked nervous, as though she wasn't sure how we'd react.

I smiled and said, "That's insane. If you'd stayed in school, you'd have your college diploma at nineteen. It would suck to have to be a grown-up when you're still a teenager."

"Thanks," she said, "but you're next."

I glared at the carpet while I admitted, "I got a twenty-three thirty on my SATs."

"What was the breakdown?" Marissa asked.

"Eight hundred verbal, eight hundred writing, seven-thirty math."

"But that's really good!" Callie said.

"You don't know Charley," Marissa explained. "They invented the A-plus just to please his parents."

Marissa's words echoed inside my head: *Just to please his parents*. And I wondered why, if I'd spent the past seventeen years of my life trying to please them, none of us seemed very happy, and not just with my SAT score. A score that I should just start to deal with because I sure as hell didn't want the stress of retesting.

"Your turn," I told Marissa.

She shook her head. "Pass."

"No fair!" Callie said. "You can't do that."

"And you can't change the rules," Marissa shot back. "When Skylar explained the game, she said we could pass if we wanted. I don't particularly want to reveal my deep dark secrets tonight, so I pass."

"Whatever," Callie said. "You're like such a freak."

"It's okay," Marissa said. "I may be a freak. Doesn't bother me. I like who I am."

"You would," Callie said darkly, stabbing her cigarette out on her plate. "Too bad you don't have taste."

"Whoa, stop it!" Skylar said.

"But she's not playing the game right!" Callie wailed.

Time to make like my future and disappear.

I reached into my backpack and pulled out my iPod. I decided on 3 Doors Down, scrolling through the playlists until I found what I was looking for. I stretched out on the ground and tried not to hear the yelling.

After half listening to one song, I took off my headphones and watched the debacle.

"Whatever!" Callie said. "You are *so* not coming with me to Marquee tonight. And you won't get in without me, because I know the promoter!"

She grabbed her purse and jammed it onto her shoulder so forcefully that I thought it was going to circle around her arm like in a cartoon.

"That's enough, Callie," Skylar said sharply. "Stop it."

"Whatever. I'm out of here. I don't need to waste my time helping you find your fucked-up friend. Say hi to your parents for me, 'kay?"

She slammed the door on her way out.

"Well," I said, trying to lighten the mood, "you keep excellent company."

"Oh, our parents have been friends since we were five. Don't mind Cal. She had a rough childhood. Her nanny raised her."

Suddenly it dawned on me what was so creepy about Callie.

"She's exactly like Blake!" I said.

Marissa frowned, and then she laughed. "You're right. Whoa, that's crazy. Female Blake sucked."

"She wasn't that bad," I said in defense of the hot blond psycho.

"You're only saying that because she's pretty," Skylar said.

"You're prettier," I replied, looking at my sneakers.

"Oh really, 'Mr. John Mayer Holding a Fuzzy Puppy Adorable?' " she mocked, her green eyes large and glittering.

"Really."

Our eyes locked into place.

It was so ridiculous. There I was, a boarding-school runaway, wearing a sweatshirt from a college I didn't want to go to, in this hotel room that belonged to a billionaire, staring at the girl I'd tried so hard not to want.

Neither of us looked away for a long time, and that was fine with me.

"When should we head uptown?" Skylar asked.

"Soon, I guess," I said.

"And if we don't find him tonight," Skylar said, "tomorrow Marissa and I can check out some of the places he mentioned in his e-mail, and then maybe you can sleuth out the NYU scene and see if we get any leads from that."

"Sure," I agreed, but we all left it unspoken that if tonight bombed, we'd be wandering around a city with no real idea where to find him.

Suddenly I was exhausted. Everything hit me at once— the heat, the immensity of what we'd done and where we were, the hopelessness of finding Blake in a city as crowded as New York, our ridiculous clues, Callie—and I yawned until my jaw popped and the nose pads on my glasses dug into the bridge of my nose with a vengeance.

"I'm tired, too," Skylar said. "I'm going to take a quick shower to wake up before we head out."

I checked the clock. It wasn't late at all.

I sighed and went to sprawl on the couch while we waited. I looked up at the chandelier on the ceiling, the crown moldings, and the little green light on the smoke detector.

"Um, Charley?" Marissa said, and I turned my head to the side and stared at her, hoping that maybe Marissa could do something. Anything. Christ, I was desperate.

"Yeah?"

I heard the water turn on in the bathroom, and I pictured the large, gleaming shower, with tiny hotel bottles of shampoo and conditioner, so much better than the life-sized Tupperware-container shower stalls we had in the Milbank Hall bathrooms.

"I know you like her."

I almost fell of the couch in surprise.

"What?"

"You mean *who*." Marissa giggled, and her pale bangs slipped out from behind her ear and dangled loose in front of her face.

"Fine. Who?"

"Skylar. Come on, Charley. It's obvious. 'You're so much cuter than Callie.' Sound familiar?"

"Well, she is."

"No shit, Sherlock. But you didn't have to tell her."

Wow. Marissa was cursing? The universe was obviously standing on its ass, farting the ABCs, as Blake used to say freshman year whenever anything was weird.

"Since when do you say 'shit'?"

"Since I decided to just try and enjoy myself."

I chuckled a little because she seemed to mean it. If nothing else, at least Marissa was genuine.

"You're crazy."

"At least I'm not in denial," she shot back.

"What, about Skylar? Come on."

"Charley, you're the one who said it. Think about *that*."

She had me. It was so goddamned unfair the way Marissa just watched everything, sponging up information.

"Skylar's the type of girl everyone likes." *Especially the Dorseys,* I left out. "I bet half the guys at Hilliard want to do her."

"But you don't," Marissa said emphatically. "I know you, Charley. You're an overachiever, not a sex fiend. You want to date Skylar, not just have sex."

"So what?" I asked, wondering where this was going.

"So she should be dating you. You'd be good for her. You'd be good for each other. You could show her that not every guy thinks with his lower brain."

"Gotcha. Much lower."

"Exactly. So you should tell her how you feel about her."

"It's not that easy."

"Why not?" Marissa tilted her head and stared at me, waiting for an answer.

"It's not like in books or plays," I tried to explain. "I'll *um* my way through a mess of words and then turn red while she wonders what the hell I'm mumbling about. And what about Blake? I can't even start to explain what kind of a betrayal it would be if he thought I'd stolen Skylar from him."

"You can talk to Blake when we find him. But it's obvious how much you like her, Charley. And doesn't Skylar have some say in this, too? I bet you'd totally woo her with some awesome speech. Give yourself a chance. You're a debate champion."

"Finalist," I corrected. "Skylar is the champion."

"It doesn't matter who's first," Marissa said fiercely. "God, I'm so sick of you guys. 'Who's going to be the valedictorian?

Who's going to be the best?' Who cares! You're both talented. The numbers shouldn't matter."

"I guess."

The water turned off.

"Promise you'll kiss her tomorrow," Marissa said, smiling. "It would be so romantic!"

"I'll do my best," I said, winking, as Skylar came out of the bathroom tying a terry hotel robe closed.

Her hair was wet and plastered to her head. She was so sexy, so perfect, and so very naked under that terry-cloth robe.

"Climb on the couch?" I asked innocently, and Skylar laughed.

"You wish. Bathroom's free if you need it before we leave."

I didn't. I closed my eyes and listened to the girls mess with their things.

We walked to the subway and shared a MetroCard, passing it back through the turnstile. Even in the night, the platform was so uncomfortably warm that the tracks seemed to waver in the heat.

The subway, when it came, was mercifully air-conditioned, and unmercifully crowded. I watched a teenage guy in a hooded sweatshirt grin as he purposely bumped into Skylar from behind.

"Sorry," he said when she turned around.

Then he did it again. I leaned over.

"Skylar, why don't you grab on to me instead of the dirty pole?"

She shot me a grateful look and wrapped an arm around my waist. The kid in the sweatshirt scowled.

Skylar rode like that all the way up to the 116th Street stop, one arm circling my waist, her leg and hip leaning into me. I was real thankful for crowded subway cars.

When we got off the subway and made it back onto the street, I stared at Columbia in awe. From the street, we could just see the backs of buildings, immense pillars, and green roofs obscured behind high iron gates.

We walked along the block. (It was Broadway, I saw on a street sign. I'd always pictured Broadway as neon lights, not cafés and bookstores like there were uptown.) The street traffic was a slow trickle, not at all the vibrant crowd of college students I'd pictured.

"How many people actually do summer session here?" I asked suspiciously.

"I don't know," Skylar admitted, as we walked through the wrought-iron gates.

The campus was different from Harvard. Everything was squeezed together, the grassy areas fenced off, the buildings looming in the darkness.

Suddenly, I realized that the three of us (or four, if Blake was nearby) would never be on a college campus together.

We wandered through the campus, then across the brick pathway and through the gates onto the next avenue, which was called Amsterdam. There was a group of five college students standing on the corner. The guys were in blazers with their jeans, and the girls wore long tops that floated in the night air like kites. They had to be dressed to go to a party. Skylar, Marissa, and I exchanged a look and decided to follow them.

We walked across the avenue and onto another part of the campus. They stopped outside a dorm building where a bunch of students were waiting at a security desk to sign in. We joined the line.

"Hey," Skylar said, tapping one of the blazered guys on the arm. "Do you know where the party is?"

"Yeah, the Philo suite. Do you need me to sign you in?"

"That would be great," Skylar said. "This is Josh's party, right?"

"I have no idea," the guy said. "Andrew invited me."

We dug for our school IDs and slapped them on the counter.

"Are you still in high school?" one of the girls asked us.

"We just graduated," I told her, thinking fast. She seemed to accept that.

Once we got inside the complex, I could see how different the dorms were from what we had at Hilliard. Everything was arranged in suites. Five names on construction-paper name tags on each door—co-ed, too. The door to one of the suites was quite literally pulsing with music. We walked inside and up a narrow staircase that led into a semiprivate common room. The walls had been painted red and movie posters for *Kill Bill* and *Fight Club* hung above regulation blue-upholstered dorm couches. The place was packed.

The kitchen counter was littered with mostly empty bottles of liquor and plastic cups. There had been pizza—now there was just a stack of greasy boxes. Someone's iPod was hooked up to an expensive Bose stereo system that was pad-locked to a bookcase.

"Is this Josh's party?" I asked one of the other guys we'd walked in with.

"I guess, if he's in Philo, dude," he told me, and I gave him a look like, *Huh?*

"Philolexian Society," one of the girls said. "They're like a literary and debating club."

"Oh, right," I said.

From the looks of the party, it didn't matter if I knew what club was throwing it or not.

Skylar grabbed my hand and dragged me through the crowd. We walked down the suite's hallway and looked into some small single rooms where students were drinking beer, listening to playlists, and watching TVs. No sign of Blake.

"Hey," Skylar called into the last room, "anybody see a guy named Blake?"

"Yeah, he just left," a girl who was smoking a cigarette said.

Skylar let go of my hand, which had suddenly gone clammy and cold. No way.

"He had to take his laundry out of the dryer," someone else called.

"What?" Skylar asked, confused.

"Blake Bennington?"

"Oh, never mind. Different Blake. Thanks."

Skylar leaned against the wall in the hallway and sighed.

"It would have been too easy," I told her.

"I guess you're right."

"We'll find him," I said.

She smiled faintly.

"I think right now we should go find Marissa."

We pushed past the crowds in the hallway and made it back into the common room. Marissa was sitting on the edge of a sofa, giggling and talking to three guys.

"Hey," Marissa said, waving. "Have you met the Philos? Andrew, Eric and, um, Lev?"

"No, I haven't," I said, shaking their hands. "This is a great party. Is there anything else happening on campus tonight, or are you guys pretty much it? I thought some guy named Josh was having something."

"Haven't heard about any more dorm parties. Although Saint A's is throwing something," one of the guys said, miming snorting coke. He laughed.

I hoped Blake wasn't there. Skylar, Marissa, and I exchanged a look.

"Crap," one of the guys on the couch said, looking at his watch. "Hey, everyone!"

He held his goblet (yes, it was an actual glass goblet) of wine in the air, and suddenly the party got real quiet.

" 'Hold fast to the spirit of youth, let years to come do what they may!' " A lot of people yelled, and then downed the contents of their cups.

I sighed. The search for Blake was majorly sucking. Suddenly I heard Foo Fighters blast from the speakers. Someone had turned up the music. Skylar started to dance, and a lot of the guys watched her.

"Marissa, do you think we should head out soon?" I asked, turning around. Marissa wasn't there.

Skylar was still dancing. She caught my eye and motioned toward the staircase. I nodded and started walking.

Marissa was leaning against the wall at the bottom of the stairs, Skylar's pink phone cradled to her chest, her own phone to her ear. For a second, I got scared that she was talking to the school administration or Mr. McCabe, or telling her overprotective parents where we were. But then a new song started on the stereo, and the intro was soft enough that I could hear what Marissa was saying.

"Hey, Kyle, it's Marissa Rodolf, Blake's friend from Hilliard. I got your number from Skylar's phone. Anyway, we found Blake's e-mail. We're in the city. If you know where he is, or if you want to help us find him, give me a call at 503-555-9168. Thanks."

When she shut the phone, Marissa looked up and saw me.

"Please don't tell Skylar," she said. "But I had a feeling she hadn't deleted his number. She's obsessive about her caller ID."

"I won't." I didn't know if it should weird me out that Skylar left the number in her phone after all this time, but I didn't really care to think about it. It's not like she was my girlfriend, or like I had any business knowing what was in her phone.

"Good," Marissa said, "because we really need Kyle's help now."

"I know. You were right to call. Come on, let's put Skylar's phone back before she notices."

When Marissa and I walked back into the common room, I glanced at the clock. It was after midnight. By the time we got downtown, it would be one in the morning.

"Hey," I asked a guy, "whatever happened to Josh's party? Isn't that every Thursday night?"

"That got shut down last week," the guy said. "Three a.m. and some kid went crazy on his girlfriend. He wrecked the suite. Josh isn't having any more parties."

"Thanks," I said.

It looked like we weren't going to find Blake that night. So the three of us ditched the party, got our IDs back from the front security desk, and decided that Blake probably wasn't hanging around Columbia after all. Our one real lead was a dead end.

13

Skylar: Vanity Unfair

When I woke up in the hotel room the next morning, for a moment I wasn't sure where I was. The distant street sounds, stories below, threw me. The blackout curtains across the entrance to the balcony kept all the light out, and there was just the faint glow of the clock, 8:52 a.m., and this *person* in bed with me, who was whispering.

"Yeah, I can meet you at eleven-thirty. Okay. See you."

Then my head cleared and I realized I was in Callie's parents' suite sharing a bed with Marissa, who was whispering into her phone.

"Who was that?" I asked, yawning.

"Oh, uh, Callie," Marissa said. "She felt bad about last night, so she's going to help me look for Blake today."

"Really?" I asked, both surprised and pleased that Callie had come around. "That's nice of her."

"Yeah. She's cool," Marissa said. "We're meeting at the Time Warner building in a place called Columbus Circle."

"I'm checking out the Upper East Side today, and the Sheep Meadow, since Blake mentioned it in the e-mail. Tag along, Mariss? It's close to Columbus Circle."

"Sure."

I climbed out of bed and took my bag into the ginormous bathroom, which was seriously the size of my dorm room at Hilliard. I kind of went overboard, putting on more makeup than usual and matching my underwear and bra because I was so excited to be back in New York. Besides, you should always dress for an unexpected adventure, even if the adventure has a grim catalyst.

As I walked out of the bathroom, I glanced at Charley on the couch. His hair was a mess, and his arm was dangling off the side. He looked . . . adorable.

"All yours," I told Marissa, smoothing the wrinkles out of my cute Marc by Marc Jacobs sundress.

"Thanks."

Marissa climbed out of bed and staggered into the bathroom in her oversized godawful Full Metal Alchemist T-shirt. After a couple of minutes, she stuck her head out of the bathroom.

"What?" I asked, looking up from my problem set. I'd been sneaking in some calc time before we left.

"I was looking for some extra towels in the closet, and I found all these clothes that someone left here."

The Minters probably left some emergency clothes in the hotel, and I told Marissa as much. Then I went to see for myself. Off the bathroom was a gigantic walk-in closet and, sure enough, it had a dozen garment bags hanging up. The first bag

I unzipped contained a gorgeous new Zac Posen silk skirt and Marni lace top. And they looked just Marissa's size.

"You should totally wear this today," I gushed, taking the skirt off the hanger and thrusting it at Marissa.

"What?" Marissa looked appalled.

"Why not? I'm sure Callie won't mind. And you guys are hanging out, anyway. She'd want you to look cute. Come on, you have to do it!"

"Actually, I don't," Marissa said. "Has it ever occurred to you that I'm happy with the way I look? Not everyone needs to look like they've stepped out of a fashion magazine."

I took a step back involuntarily and felt my spine pressing against the cold full-length mirror.

"Whoa, I'm sorry," I said. And I was sorry. "I wasn't trying to force you to change who you are. I just thought it might be fun to play dress-up in a four-hundred-dollar skirt."

"Well, wearing things I can't afford isn't my idea of fun." Marissa looked at her feet, then added, "I'm sorry. I've just been really jumpy ever since we left Hilliard. Forget it. I didn't mean to snap at you."

"I didn't mean to make you snap," I said.

Then I gave Marissa a big hug. I'd never realized that by not caring about fashion, she was making her own fashion statement. Even though we'd been friends since ninth grade, I'd never really felt like I understood Marissa, but now I was starting to.

I figured we'd walk the Upper East Side, then I'd hang around Central Park and try to strike up a conversation with some local kids, maybe find out what parties were going on. I could stake out the Sheep Meadow while Marissa went off with Callie.

In the hotel elevator, I pulled out my cell phone and called Charley.

Four rings.

"Whuhhh," Charley moaned.

"I knew you were still sleeping—I knew it! Wake up, Charley!"

"Hi, Skylar." He yawned. "Where are you?"

"We just left. Time to wake up and get started searching for Blake."

"It's early."

"Everyone at school is in morning assembly. They don't think it's early."

"Yes they do." I could hear Charley yawn again. "And they didn't have to spend the night on a couch."

"Complain, complain, complain. Just get up. You have a busy day ahead of you checking out the party scene at NYU. And I'll text you every five minutes if I have to, so there's no way you're going back to sleep."

"Unnnnnh. I'm up. Talk to you later."

I snapped my phone shut and stepped out of the elevator. The doorman tried to hail a cab for Marissa and me, but I knew the subway would be faster.

When we got to the Upper East Side, I knew where we had to go first. I needed to see it for myself, the building I'd wished every day in Westchester County that we'd never left.

I followed my feet to my old block toward Madison Avenue. Marissa and I were both silent, helplessly pulled into the solemnity of my mission. And then suddenly we were there.

The creamy limestone façade glistened in the sunlight, matching the ivory trim on the green canopy that led into the lobby. The building stretched upward for two dozen stories, the right angle of each corner softened by jutting glass balconies.

A well-put-together woman in nautical Ralph Lauren and her young daughter, wearing a daisy-colored sundress, with her hair in pigtails, got out of a cab and walked toward the door. I watched a doorman I didn't recognize open the door for them, greeting them by name with a smile.

"This is it?" Marissa asked.

I nodded. I had taken her home with me to Tarrytown for Thanksgiving when we were freshmen, and it was strange knowing that Marissa could piece my life together now—my life separate from the one I had at Hilliard.

"Which was your apartment?" she asked.

"That one," I said, pointing toward a set of windows without balconies in the middle of the sixth floor.

Mom's agency hadn't had such successful clients back then, and the two-bedroom apartment, the neighborhood, and my schooling had all been a stretch.

We stood there for a moment longer before I turned and walked toward Fifth Avenue, Marissa following. The immense steps of the Metropolitan Museum were on our right, dusted with tourists all carrying the same Poland Spring water bottles they'd bought at the hot dog cart on the corner. A few banners hung above the entrance advertising the new exhibitions. We continued walking down the evil, shoe-slaughtering cobblestones next to Central Park, making our way toward the Fifth Avenue department stores.

I loved being in the city. Thank God Blake hadn't run away to somewhere boring, like New Hampshire or Maine, because I so wouldn't have gone after him. Well, I would have—I just wouldn't have enjoyed it.

I looked up while I walked, thinking about the pent-houses, wishing my parents hadn't bought the house in Tarrytown when I was nine, pulled me out of Dalton, and bought an SUV.

I wondered what my life would be like if I'd stayed in the city and moved in with the Minters (who were never home anyway and probably wouldn't have noticed me for a year). Would I have dyed my hair Bergdorf blond, gone to charity galas, and searched eagerly for my friends in the society pages? The possibilities, or "almost Skylars," as I liked to think of them, were limitless.

I flagged down a cab for Marissa, and then I walked through the park, staring up at the elaborate rooftop gardens that were visible above the trees. I remembered this park from my childhood. Callie and I would come here with her nanny and feed the ducks leftover French bread. I was going to find Blake. I knew it. I walked the rest of the way to the Sheep Meadow in a blur of sound and introspection and hopefulness.

The Sheep Meadow stretched on for acres, a huge expanse of grass littered with beach towels, folding chairs, and girls in Chanel sunglasses. Some guys my age were chucking a football around, but I knew without looking that Blake wasn't one of the Izod-poloed football tossers.

My heel got caught in the grass and I stumbled slightly, planting a foot squarely on a girl's towel.

"Sorry," I said. "I nearly fell off my shoe."

The girl looked like she was my age. She gave me the once-over, head to toe, before she accepted my apology.

"No problem. Hey, do you go to Brearley?"

"Not even," I returned. "Hilliard."

"Oh. I thought you looked like someone's friend from this party."

"Doubtful."

I gave this girl the once-over back, taking in her too-trendy, had-to-be-six-dollars-from-H&M bikini top and linen shorts. She had parked her towel parallel to two friends'.

"I'm Cordelia," the girl said, flipping her shoulder-length hair. She didn't bother to introduce her friends.

"Nice to meet you. I'm Skylar."

"Do you live around here?" she asked.

"No. I used to, though. I was at Dalton for a while."

"Then you must have known Selena Parker-Owens," she said.

The name didn't ring a bell, or trigger any memories of Page Six mentions. I told her as much.

"Oh, well, she was no Callie Minter, but we grew up across the hall from each other."

"I'm friends with Callie," I said.

She lit up like a vanity mirror, her eyes glittering. "Really?"

she asked. "I've never had the time to stop by one of her SoHo Grand suite parties, but I hear they're insane."

"I wouldn't know," I said, "but I've got the suite on loan for the next few days."

"No way!" Cordelia practically lost it. "Is there really a twenty-foot spa and a private roof deck?"

"Sure, honey," I said, rolling my eyes. If I had told her that the closets had rotating racks like at the dry cleaner's, and that every book on the shelves was about Euclidean geometry and Eigenvectors, she would have believed me too.

"Actually," I said, "I was wondering if you could help me out. You seem to know everyone. I'm looking for a friend of mine who's in town. A friend of *Callie's*."

I stressed the connection, even though it was a lie. I figured it would make an impact on her, and it did. She sat up and stared at me in rapture.

"Blake Dorsey," I told her. "Have you seen him?"

"In New York Social Diary?" she asked, confused.

"Not exactly. Just around the city. Here, maybe? Or at a party?"

She wrinkled her nose and looked at her crew, the silent, sullen not-Cordelia girls, who shrugged.

"Nope. Hey, maybe he'll be at that party tonight that what's-her-face is throwing."

"Do you know where it is?"

"Oh, some town house," Cordelia said, shrugging, and I clenched my hands into fists of frustration. "I was invited, of course, but I'm just far too busy to attend."

"Naturally," I said dryly. "But none of you remember where it is or who's throwing it?"

"Sorry," one of the not-Cordelias said, flipping a page of her *US Weekly*.

"But hey," Cordelia said, "you should take my cell number. Maybe you and Callie would want to meet up with us later for Bellinis? She's a member at Cipriani Upstairs, right? I mean, she can get us in?"

"Probably," I said. "And I'd love your number."

I programmed her into my phone under "Social Climber."

Cordelia grinned, as though anticipating texting all her friends that the blond magazine heiress of the Upper East Side was taking her to Cipriani Upstairs.

God. Maybe it was a good thing I didn't stay in New York. I might have turned into Cordelia. Or worse, a not-Cordelia.

"Omigod," one of the not-Cordelias squealed, "they're coming over!"

"Who?" I asked, but then I saw what she was talking about.

The guys who had been tossing the football around were walking in our direction. Their football was on the grass about ten feet away from us. I walked over and picked it up, feeling the rough bumps of the ball pressing into my fingers like Braille.

"You lose this?" I asked.

There were four guys, all with that rakish, summers-on-the-Cape look. They seemed a little bit younger than I was, maybe fifteen or sixteen.

"Thanks," the tallest one said. "Toss it over."

"I would," I said, "but I just got my nails done and don't want to chip them. Come over here." I shot a look at Cordelia and her crew, who watched in amazement as I was suddenly surrounded by four hot guys.

Now that I had them, I was going to get the information from them that I couldn't get from Cordelia.

"So are you going to that party tonight?" I asked. "The one in the town house?"

"Maybe," one of the guys said. "I never know about those things in advance."

"Yeah," another one said, "he just gets the calls from his girlfriend—'Come over in half an hour'—and finds out if they're going anywhere when he sees whether or not she's wearing any clothes."

They laughed. I made a face. *Ewww. Grow up.*

"So no plans at all for tonight?" I probed, handing over the football.

One of the guys shrugged. "Xbox?"

"Well, I'll leave you to it," I said, walking away.

Cordelia waved vigorously when I passed her, but I didn't stop. I couldn't go around interviewing every teenager on the Sheep Meadow. It was pointless. Maybe I could meet up with Charley and we could check out the area around NYU together. Or maybe I needed a better plan.

I came out on the other side of the park, Central Park West, and grabbed a subway downtown. If Blake was here, he wasn't necessarily staying with his friend. Maybe he checked into a hotel, and I could find him that way.

I got off the train near Washington Square Park and

ransacked the travel shelves in the Barnes & Noble for guides to New York City budget hotels and accommodations. I took my armload of books into the café, burned my tongue on a venti hot chocolate, pulled out my cell phone, dialed the first listing under A, and asked to be connected to Mr. Dorsey's room.

14

Charley: Much Ado About NYU

The city felt right to me from the moment I stepped out the door of the hotel and onto the sidewalk. The sticky, flickering heat enveloped me and I stopped in some store to ask for directions to NYU.

It was liberating, actually, having all this free time. There was no homework to do, no studying, no SAT prep, no adults breathing down my neck. I just needed to find Blake.

Washington Square Park was quite literally a square of towering buildings around a park, and I felt at home there, more so than at Harvard. There were purple NYU flags flying from the buildings, just simple letters named after a place, not a person and his legacy.

The crowds on the sidewalks looked different than they did near Grand Central. Pretty much everyone was young, pierced and messenger-bagged to within an inch of their lives.

I was hungry after walking so many blocks that I'd lost count, so I ducked into a coffee place the first chance I got.

As I stood in line to order, I wondered if I should take the NYU tour, sit through an information session. Then I could get a free map of the campus and find out where the hangouts were and which were the party dorms. I could learn enough to limit the list of places Blake would go, that was, if he was here.

"What can I do you for?" the guy at the counter asked. He was wearing a purple NYU cap.

"Bottled water and an orange muffin, please," I said.

The radio station that was playing in the café started a Deep Purple song, and I absently formed the power chords with my left hand and nodded to the beat while I waited for my breakfast.

"I like this song, too," the guy said, ringing up the food. "To think we're Perfect Strangers."

I laughed.

"Yeah, but that's only because you're standing Purpendicular to me," I joked, playing along with inserting random Deep Purple album titles into our conversation.

"What's your major?" the guy asked. "You at Tisch?"

"No." I shook my head. "I'm a high school senior. What's your major?"

"Music technology. I want to produce music, you know, work on scoring for film and multimedia. That sort of thing."

I handed him a five-dollar bill and asked, "So NYU has that stuff?"

"Well, let's put it this way: it's only the best school in the country for people who want to work with music, that's all."

"You know," I said, suddenly realizing that I did want to check NYU out, and not just because Blake might be there,

"I was, uh, in the city looking for a friend, but maybe, um, do you have a class today?"

"Interested in the MT program, huh?" He grinned. "It's not just about playing instruments. That's how I got into it, though. There's recording engineering, production, post-production, scoring, software development. I have a post-prod class this afternoon, if you want to sit in."

"What time?"

"One, so you should probably meet me back here at twelve-thirty."

"Thanks."

I grabbed my food and was halfway out of the café when the guy behind the counter called, "Wait! I'm Nick."

"Charley," I said. "Later."

I ate my breakfast on one of the benches in the square, watching the people and thinking about how I got this city much more than Boston.

After a while, I asked a girl in an NYU T-shirt if she knew where the Office of Admissions was, and she pointed at a building across the park.

An information session was going to start a couple of minutes after I got there, and there was hardly any room to wait outside of the building. I stood by myself, practically the only one there who hadn't come with a parent, and generally felt hot and self-conscious and weird. When the doors opened and we went in, I headed to the back, which I never did.

I usually sat in the front of a room. That way I managed to convince myself that it was just me and the teacher, so I better do everything perfectly or else. But today I felt like staring at the backs of people's heads and knowing I didn't have to be perfect.

A man with a goatee and a faded work shirt walked to the front of the room. He took the microphone off its little stand and pulled down a projector screen.

I didn't know what to expect. I thought maybe we'd watch slides with statistics about median SAT score and class rank. But that's not what happened next—not even close.

A bunch of college kids came down the aisles and passed out glossy NYU booklets. I flipped through mine for a minute, and there were all these photos of laughing, smiling, ethnically diverse Gap-ad people running around Manhattan, climbing out of taxis, lounging in dorm rooms, typing on PowerBooks in lecture halls.

The man in the front of the room introduced himself as John something, senior admissions counselor. It couldn't be true. I'd spent practically my whole life being scared shitless of admissions counselors, thinking they were distinguished, gray-bearded academics in tweed jackets, but he was just an average guy in Adidas sneakers and black-framed rocker glasses.

While John talked, I was acutely aware that there was something missing from his speech, but for the first ten minutes, I couldn't place it.

"Now I'd like to talk with you about academics," John said, switching the microphone from his right hand to his left.

That was when I realized what the something was: studying. I'd heard all about NYU's dining facilities, dorms, clubs, internship opportunities, semester-abroad programs, and discount theater tickets, but nothing about studying.

Was college really supposed to be about more than just another four years of straight A's? Apparently, although no one had bothered to tell me until now. I didn't understand how I'd missed it. Sure, I'd heard about fraternities and college bars and *College Girls Gone Wild* DVDs, but I'd always thought it was a load of crap, the type of stories parents let their kids believe to motivate them to work their asses off in high school. Like Santa Claus. If a kid didn't give his parents hell all year, he'd get one morning's worth of presents. That's what I had always believed.

But as I sat there in that crowded lecture room listening, I finally realized that those stories I'd always heard were true. Hard work really did pay off. A 4.0 was rewarded, and a 4.5 doubly so. College was the new American dream.

While I was thinking about this and pretty much realizing that college was actually supposed to be fun, rather than an obligation to dear old M&D fulfilled, the room went dark and we all watched a video.

It wasn't about SAT scores, grades, and class rank, either. Instead, four students spoke about their experiences in the different schools at NYU while a montage of city life images flashed onscreen along with soft rock music.

After the tape ended, the lights came on again and everyone was asked to step outside to meet their tour guides. I watched, amused as hell, as some of the more determined parents jockeyed for position to ask the man with the microphone questions. I could picture my parents doing the same thing, only they would have come prepared with typed sheets of questions. I was glad to be alone.

I walked outside and stood in a small group of teenagers and families who were all waiting for the tour guide. This one girl with retro-looking glasses and a messenger bag covered in Hot Topic pins kept staring at me, so I smiled and said hi.

"Are you the tour guide?" she finally asked.

"No."

"Oh. Then where are your parents?"

For a second, I seriously considered making up an identity, playing a role like New York was my stage and I wasn't a boarding-school runaway but an actor in Schwartz Theater, but then I realized I just didn't have the energy for that.

"I came by myself."

"Cool. So do you know what you want to study?" the girl persisted.

"For sure," I said, glad that I had an answer ready that I genuinely believed in (and that would piss off my parents in a major way). "I want to major in music technology. How about you?"

"Oh, I don't even want to go here," the girl told me as though she was divulging some spectacular secret. Maybe she was. Her mother was standing ten feet away, watching. The girl leaned in close and whispered, "I want to study psychology. Even if I get into NYU, I'm still going to go to Barnard, because it's a better program. Besides, I think I'll have more fun there, with an actual campus."

I couldn't believe it. Had everyone but me figured out

what college was really about? And were their parents okay with them making their own decisions about where they wanted to spend the next four years of their lives?

I thought about this all through the tour, given by some perky girl named Tina, who had a nose ring. As I walked around Manhattan with a group of kids and their supportive parents, I felt pretty awful that my parents had no idea they weren't supporting me when they bragged to everyone that I was only ten years away from my Harvard PhD.

I vowed to call Dad after I sat in on Nick-from-the-café's music technology class. The class had been incredible, and the professor had stayed after for a few minutes to answer any questions I might have. After I explained to Nick about Blake, Nick took my number and promised to call if he heard of any huge parties that night. I put his number into my phone, and as I was about to put my cell away, I knew if I didn't call my dad then and there, I'd probably never do it.

I walked back into the park, sat down on a bench, and dialed.

I kind of hoped my dad wouldn't pick up and I could leave a voice mail that was all "IwannagotoNYUnotHarvardsorryI-hatemedicineandlovemusic."

"Charley, good to hear from you."

Crap. Why couldn't he have been on the T, where he didn't get reception, or something?

"Hi, Dad."

"To what do I owe the pleasure of this call?"

"Uh, well, here's the thing . . ."

"What's going on, son?"

"Just hear me out, okay? I mean, don't interrupt me or anything. Promise?"

"I promise. Is this about your grades?"

"No, Dad. Come on. You know I would never mess up like that."

"Then what is it?"

It was then or never.

"You know how I always liked to give speeches and act and stuff?"

"Of course. Your mom and I are proud of you, Charley. You've got that first-place International Extemporaneous trophy in the bag for this year's state tournament."

"Sure, Dad. Okay, so here's the thing. I was never that good at biology or pre-calc, right?"

"You earned solid A's."

"But I got a four on my AP bio exam."

I could almost hear Dad wincing on his end of the line. That had just about killed him. Harvard only took 5's.

"I've been thinking a lot. I don't want to do pre-med. I suck at science, and besides, I don't want to be a doctor. I just think I'm more cut out for a liberal arts education."

I heard my dad sigh as he took this news in, and I thought about how my head had started spinning when I saw Blake passed out, about how Skylar had had to take charge when we got him back to the dorm.

"I don't understand. Charley, you've always had this plan. Hilliard. Harvard. Med school. What changed?"

"See, about that plan . . . it wasn't mine."

I stared at my sneakers as I sat on the bench in Washington Square Park, and I tried to work up the confidence to say to my father what I'd been itching to tell him ever since he made me take a practice SAT test as a seventh grader, just to see if I was on the "right track."

"I have a plan of my own. I want to go to NYU and study music technology—to work on scoring for films and shows. Music is what makes me happy. And NYU is a really good school. I want to live in New York City. I've had enough of New England. Harvard is too much like Hilliard—too much of you and not enough of me. So that's what I want."

A long pause.

"I'm shocked, Charley. I had no idea you felt this way."

"That's because you never once asked me what I wanted to be when I grew up. And I never had the guts to tell you."

"Well, I'm sorry I didn't realize that you weren't as interested in medicine now as you seemed to be when you were younger. But you might change your mind. Everyone changes majors in college. You might be adamant about getting a liberal arts degree now, but you're young."

"Dad, come on. I'm not going to suddenly fall in love with organic chemistry when I turn twenty."

"Anything's possible. Maybe you'll have put all this NYU nonsense behind you by November and still apply early decision to Harvard."

"I won't, Dad. Stop."

My father sighed again. "Listen, Charley. We'll have to

talk more about this. I have a lunch meeting I need to be at, and we can't resolve this all today. But just so we're clear: if we consider NYU as one of your college options, that doesn't mean your grades and test scores can slide. Always be the best, son."

"I know. I will."

"Call your mother later. And talk to Ben. You're his brother."

"Okay. Bye, Dad."

"Love you, son."

I snapped my phone shut and stared at the little flashing call time display in shock. For the first time in my life, I'd actually had a real conversation with my father and told him how I felt. And he'd listened. It wasn't going to be the end of this—I had a feeling my dad wasn't going to give up on Ivy League colleges, where AMA stood for American Medical Association, not American Music Awards—but at least it was a start.

This day was turning out differently than I'd imagined. I'd meant for it to be about Blake, but I'd gotten caught up in my own stuff.

I took out my phone again and called Blake's cell. It went straight to voice mail.

"Blake, it's Charley. Come on, man. Skylar and I have left you a dozen messages. Call us back. We're worried, and we want to know where you are and if you're okay. We need to talk. You misunderstood everything. We're in the city, and we're looking for you. Anyway, later."

I called Skylar. Maybe she'd found something.

"Hey, you!" she answered on the first ring.

"Any luck?"

"No, how about you?"

"If I'm having any, it isn't the good kind."

"We have to find him, Charley."

"I know. I'm trying. I met a guy who promised to call me when he finds out what's going on around NYU tonight, and I have a map of all the buildings. Anyway, you won't believe what I've been up to. Where are you?"

"Walk up Washington Square East and turn right."

"Why?"

"There's a Barnes & Noble. I'm in the café. Get your butt over here, I'm lonely."

I had this huge grin on my face as I walked quickly along the sidewalk. If I didn't think about Blake, everything rocked. I'd taken a tour of the perfect college for me, sat in on a class that I was interested in taking, and finally told my father how I felt.

I was jazzed. For once my life was coalescing into something decent, instead of just one big Ivy League blur.

Skylar was waiting for me in a café, and goddammit I wanted to walk in there and kiss her—even though Blake would kill us. I liked Skylar so much, but Blake liked her, too. I couldn't betray my roommate. Not now. Not unless I knew Skylar felt the same way about me.

I walked into the Barnes & Noble and made my way toward the café, smiling when I saw her. I took the empty seat at the table. Skylar was buried behind half a dozen guides to Manhattan on a budget, cell phone and pen at the ready, a notepad full of crossed-out names of hotels.

"Mr. Dorsey isn't listed as a guest? My mistake. Thank you. Bye."

She hung up the phone and rolled her eyes.

"That's hotel number five thousand that Blake isn't staying at."

"You called five thousand hotels?" I asked skeptically.

"Well, maybe seventy-five."

"And no luck?"

"Nope. How'd you do?"

"Well, but not with the Blake thing. I kind of got sidetracked. I sat through the information session at NYU, and I took a tour and sat in on a class."

"No way!"

"For real. And I found this department I'm into, music technology—"

"I don't believe it!"

"What?"

"The great Charles Morton the Third is actually considering a music program at a school where he isn't a legacy?"

Her green eyes were huge and mocking. She didn't mean it, I surmised, but then again, she sort of did.

"That's right. And—this is the part you really won't believe—I called my dad and told him."

"What'd he say?"

"That I'll probably change my mind and transfer to Harvard, but that he'll consider letting me apply."

"That's fantastic!"

She squealed and got up from her chair, coming over to my seat and throwing her arms around me.

"I think that's so wonderful," she said in midhug, her breath tickling my neck.

"You do?"

"Of course, Charley. I care about you and—"

"I care about you, too," I blurted out. Then I realized what I'd said, and turned bright red.

Skylar and I just stared at each other, and I didn't know who was more embarrassed.

That wasn't how I'd wanted it to happen. Why wasn't she saying anything? I was screwed.

"Oh wow," Skylar said. "I don't know what I—you—and all this stuff . . ."

She looked away.

"Skylar, listen," I said, having no idea where I was going or why I was still talking, "you know how we've been battling it out for valedictorian since freshman year, and how I always still liked you? That's because it's hard not to. You loan me books and watch out for Marissa and wear shoes that make your legs look fifty feet long. If anyone has to be better than me at everything, I'm glad it's you. And I don't even mind. I just like you, Skylar. I like you a lot."

I finished my speech staring at my hands, too afraid to look up at her. But then Skylar asked, "Are you going to kiss me now, or what?"

"That depends what you thought of my speech," I said, daring myself to smile a little.

"Picket fence."

That was the debate term for perfect.

I leaned in to kiss her, to actually kiss *Skylar Banks*.

It wasn't a video game, or a song, or a chapter of some book I was reading. It wasn't a movie or a college admissions essay or even one of Marissa's poems. It was real, and it was incredible.

15

Skylar: Far from the Madison Avenue Crowd

If someone had told me a few months ago that I'd be making out with Charley Morton in New York City, I would have rolled my eyes and laughed. *Yeah, right. And those free iPod ads on the Internet are actually real.*

But in that Barnes & Noble, I realized that Charley didn't just make the perfect guy friend—he had potential to be the perfect boyfriend. He was so cute, smiling about that music program at NYU, and I was glad to be the one he shared his excitement with.

Our kisses were so powerful that I was sure they could have caused a natural disaster somewhere in the Congo. Charley was a little slow to get his hands right, but when he finally did we just got lost in each other.

When we pulled apart, his eyes were still closed, and I could see his long, dark lashes resting on his cheeks.

All of a sudden it was like the city began to fast-forward

around us and the next thing I remember after the hug was buying a MetroCard to get back to the hotel.

I looked over at Charley when we were sitting in the subway car together, thankful for the air-conditioning that had been conspicuously absent on the platform. He slipped his hand into mine and squeezed. Even when I turned away to look at the map on the wall, I could still see him in my mind, glasses and collared shirt, jeans and oversized leather wristwatch, designer sneakers and dimples.

Once we were both out of the station, we raced back to the hotel, running around the people dragging briefcases, the tourists with their Frommer's guides, and the nannies pushing strollers.

"Stop," I panted, trying to catch my breath. "We can't go into the hotel like this."

"Okay," Charley said, grandly sweeping his arm into a passing businesswoman's messenger bag, "after you, then."

We walked quietly into the lobby and to the elevator, where we waited, a perfect model of decorum. Of course, the second we were alone in the elevator, we went insane.

Charley kept trying to tickle me and I kept trying to kiss him and we fell all over each other laughing.

When I reached into my back pocket to get the room key, though, I started to wonder what would happen in five minutes, or ten minutes. Would Marissa be in the room? Would Charley and I stare at each other for an hour in uncomfortable silence? Or would we, well, get it on?

"Marissa?" I called, stepping into the room. It looked empty, but the place was so huge, I couldn't really tell.

"It's just you and me, I guess," Charley said, slipping his sneakers off by the door.

I stared at him, trying to figure out if this was a pre-coital maneuver or if he was just sick of wearing shoes. I decided it was the latter. So I took off my heels and kicked them under a chair, because suddenly I was sick of wearing shoes, too.

Charley walked over to one of the windows and I watched him press his forehead against the glass, leaning forward so his bare heels lifted off the floor.

"What are you doing?"

"I don't know," he said, "just looking. When I stare at the city, I see all these people. So I pick one person out of the crowd and think about them. I wonder what their life is like."

"Did you ever do that at Hilliard?" I asked.

"Yeah, I did. I used to pick you out of the crowd all the time."

"And what did you think about?"

"How I wanted to kiss you."

Charley stood up straight, and I got the impression that he was praying so hard in the back of his mind for me to kiss him at that moment that I did. It felt like fireworks in triplicate! So amazing.

We kept kissing until my breath was coming in hard gasps and my stomach was pressing against Charley's belt. The only thing I could think to do was push against him until he took a few steps backward and wound up with his legs against the bed frame.

Practically everything was running through my mind while we were lip-locked. I was thinking about what time it was, and whether or not I had to pee, and whether or not I'd shaved above my knees the night before, and whether Charley was wearing boxers or briefs. But mostly I was thinking that I was living up to the slut reputation I'd tried so hard to overcome.

Charley noticed my hesitation, and he gave me a kiss on the cheek.

"Hey, sit down a sec, okay?"

He pulled me down so we were sitting next to each other on the edge of the bed.

"I don't want you to regret anything, so I'm fine with whatever you want to do," Charley told me, his hand on my back. "I'm not just looking for a random hookup. You don't have to worry about that."

"I know," I said, and then, gratefully, "Thanks."

"Come here, you," he whispered, smiling at me. That was when I realized Charley was one of those sideways kissers. He wasn't aggressive enough to be on top, and he didn't trust himself with me lying on top of him, so we were taco-ed together, instead of making a human sandwich. Way to think outside the bun.

We kissed and kissed until I was firmly under the impression that kissing was *all* Charley knew how to do. It was up to me to teach him the ways of the world, so I sort of pressed myself against him sideways and started rubbing his lower back under his T-shirt. He reciprocated. I grabbed his hand and pulled it around to my front.

Charley's hand stopped moving, unsure of where it was

allowed to venture. "It's okay," I told him, and he shot his hand up my top so fast that I practically bit his tongue off laughing.

How could I have known him for three years and never felt like this before? How could I have wasted my time with horny-as-hell jock-boy Kyle? I mean, anyone whose social label was named after a type of strap couldn't embody the qualities I was looking for in a man.

Then, of course, I told myself to shut up, because I wasn't supposed to be cracking mental jokes while fooling around. And of course since I told myself to stop, I couldn't. As I pulled my top off, I said, "Fooling around is like a debate tournament: You never know what position you'll wind up in."

Charley chuckled a little, but I could see that he didn't really want to hear any more jokes. Trying to get my brain to quiet down, I leaned over and unbuttoned the two little buttons on his polo shirt, at that moment finding the little polo person straddling the horse in the logo to be sexually explicit as hell.

Charley yanked his top over his head in one fluid motion that left his hair tousled—perfect for me to run my fingers through and smooth down.

But just as I patted the last hair into place and we were topless, the door opened.

My first thought was, not again!

"Skylar? Charley?" Marissa called from the L-shaped entryway.

Charley froze with his hands all over my chest, and I pushed him away quickly, trying to find my top. Had I flung it somewhere?

I got out of the bed and quickly dropped onto all fours beside it, looking under the bed. No top. Shit. I grabbed Charley's shirt off the corner of the bed and slipped it on.

"Marissa?" I called, standing up and tugging the top down. "We're both here."

"I know where he is!" Marissa yelled, slamming the front door and taking a running leap onto one of the sofas.

"What?" I asked. "Callie found him?"

"I wasn't out with Callie," Marissa said, grinning. "I only told you I was because I knew you'd be upset."

"Why would I be upset?" I demanded coolly, raising an eyebrow.

"Charley?" Marissa appealed.

"No way. You tell her," he said.

"You're in on this little don't-tell-Skylar conspiracy, too?" I asked, scandalized. What was going on?

"I got a number out of your phone last night," Marissa said. "I called Kyle—"

"You did *what*?" I yelled. "Marissa!"

She shrugged. "It worked, didn't it?"

"That remains to be proven," I said.

"Then Kyle called me back this morning and asked me to meet him at Columbus Circle. So I told you I was going to see Callie."

"I can't believe this," I said, sitting down on the edge of

the sofa. Charley poked me in the back gently with his toe, and I glared at him. I wasn't in the mood for his cute antics.

"I'm sorry," Marissa said. "I didn't know what else to do. Blake sent that e-mail to Kyle, so I figured he was part of this, too. And I was right. Blake is staying on the Upper West Side with that girl, Sara, from the blog, and Kyle is there, too. Apparently, their families used to vacation together, so Kyle still had Sara's cell number. When he got Blake's e-mail, he made a few calls and found out Blake had showed up at Sara's doorstep reeking of whiskey and carrying a duffel bag."

"So Blake's okay?" I asked.

Marissa shrugged. "Not really. Kyle tried to talk to him, but he didn't think it helped. Blake and Sara are throwing a party tonight. Kyle knows it's a bad idea, but at least it means Blake won't be leaving the house."

"Let me guess," I said wryly, trying to change the subject from Kyle. "Is the party bring your own casserole? Or is he going with the Tupperware theme?"

Charley stood up, hands thrust deep into the pockets of his jeans, and I got a good look at him without his shirt. Yum. Why couldn't Marissa have waited ten more minutes before interrupting us?

"What time should we get there?" Charley asked.

"It's an open house," Marissa said. "Kyle said ten or eleven. He'll be hanging around making sure things don't get too out of hand, and we're free to force Blake to come back to the hotel and then drag him back to Hilliard."

"You did good, Marissa," I said. I meant it. She had been

right to call Kyle. I should have had the nerve, but I was glad Marissa had been the one to do it. She was grinning, so proud of herself. And I was proud of her, too.

"So what did you two do today?" Marissa asked.

"Ugh, Sheep Meadow," I said, rolling my eyes. "And my thumbs are sore. I must have called a thousand hotels and asked for Dorsey."

"I tried my luck at NYU," Charley said. "I actually really like it there. I think I'm going to apply, and not as a safety."

"They have a good pre-med program, I guess," Marissa said.

Charley grinned. "They have an even better music program."

Marissa raised her eyebrows. "Whoa. Awesome. So, uh, Skylar . . . why are you wearing Charley's shirt?"

"Charley and I were, like, hugging. And it was the freakiest thing because when we pulled apart, we were wearing each other's clothes, y'know?"

"Uh-huh, sure." Marissa smiled. "It's okay with me, though. I had a feeling."

"How?" I asked.

"I guessed. And I'm glad you two went for it. Just as long as you didn't go *all the way* for it."

"Not even. Although thanks a lot for walking in on us."

Marissa shrugged. "Sorry. But it's not like it hasn't happened to you before."

"Hey!" I screeched in mock outrage, but then I sighed and said, "You're right. God, my life is like a syllogism. If I kiss a boy, then we get walked in on."

"Only you would think of kissing me in mathematical terms," Charley said, leaning in to kiss me again.

When his lips met mine, I felt better about having to see Kyle, more sure about convincing Blake to change, and happier with my decision to let a boy into my life than I'd ever been before.

16

Charley: Partying Is Such Sweet Sorrow

Blake's party was in a town house on the Upper West Side. As we looked for the address Skylar was clomping down West End Avenue in a short skirt and these giant heels that made her legs look like the sexiest things I'd ever seen in my life.

I wondered if I'd get to make out with Skylar again that night, if that would be taking it slow enough. And if Marissa would interrupt us again, which would majorly suck because it seemed like we had been going somewhere good earlier.

While I was trying to figure this out, we passed a side street and I heard this awful music.

"I think I know where the party is," Marissa said dryly.

We made it to the front door of this four-story miniature house, and before I could knock, Skylar rolled her eyes and pushed the door open.

The first impression I had of the house party was that it was a jumble of the things I'd stayed away from ever since "high" stopped being the opposite of "low" back in the seventh grade. There was the noise of kids talking on cell phones, blasting music, and other drunken bullshit. There was the smell of countless sweating bodies from mad dancing, too much booze, or physical contact. Not like I objected to physical contact. I just preferred to be sober so I could remember every glorious moment of it the next morning.

"Hey, I don't want us to lose each other, so let's—" I looked behind me and realized Skylar and Marissa had disappeared. I was on my own.

Blake had to be there somewhere. How could he not be at his own party? I decided to check the kitchen. Where the hell was the kitchen? I went up a flight of stairs, dodging the kids who were sprawled over the old wooden steps. Kitchen, kitchen—aha, kitchen!

There were two kegs on top of the granite counter, and a bunch of guys were clustered around them, playing some stupid drinking game.

"Hump her!" one of the guys yelled, and I stood there wondering if I'd actually heard someone give that command.

"I said," a guy slurred, leaning into my face so I could smell his beer breath, "do ya wanna play thumper?"

"Oh, no thanks," I said.

I went through a pair of swinging doors and entered a dining room with a table that was as long as a subway car. It was fully set, and five girls were relaxing in the chairs and smoking cigarettes. They had the good alcohol, I guess, because they were drinking out of crystal tumblers.

"Hi!" this tall brunette chick squealed. "Wha'sh your name?"

"Uh, I'm Charley," I told her.

"Wow, tha'sh a sexy name." She exhaled this disgusting nicotine-laden smoke at me. "I'm Sara, and you're my new boyfrien'. Your firs' job ish to pour me summore Campari."

Jesus, she was drunk off her ass.

"For sure," I told her, wondering which bottle in the extensive unlocked liquor cabinet was Campari, and how I could get out of this little club meeting Sara and her friends were having.

"You've heard of Charlie'sh Angels, right?" Sara said. "Omigod, we can be, like, your angels."

"Fantastic," I muttered. "Hey, I have to head out. I'm looking for this guy, Blake—"

"Everybody'sh looking for Blake." She pouted. "But nobody'sh looking for me. Is thish a good party?" She tottered toward me, wobbling on high heels, and placed her arms around my neck.

"Oh, yeah, sure," I said, not wanting to hurt her feelings.

"Because I give the best parties. I'm famous for them. Mine are the best. I give the best something elsh, too. Want one?"

Good God, she was *not* talking about what I thought she was talking about. I didn't want that. I'd just discovered the kissing-with-hands maneuver this afternoon. Plus, I wanted fooling around to be like chord progressions: you had to master the basics before you got into the harder stuff. And, furthermore, she said this was her party. Either she was *really* drunk, or this was Blake's friend, i.e., bad news.

"Wow, that would be . . ."

"Super. Turn around."

What? She sort of forced me around and then started massaging my neck. It felt annoying, because her nails kept digging into my collar.

"Aren't my back rubs great?"

"Yeah. This sure makes the party rocking," I told her half-heartedly, relieved she hadn't been offering a blow job.

"I told you. This party ish the social event of the summer. Summer's so lonely. Nothing to do." She laughed and dropped her hands to my lower back. "Not like there ever is. And no parents to tell us what we can't do. I think mine are in Fransh. God, I'm so *bored*!"

That's when her hands shot around my waist and started fumbling at my belt.

"Sara, what are you doing?" I asked her.

"Ish okay, my friends will leave us alone."

It was then that I heard this roar of drunken laughter come from the kitchen. No way. Not even if the girl was cute and willing as hell. It was insane. I was jailbait, she was drunk and horny, and I didn't want to be a part of it. I wanted Skylar. I couldn't screw up monogamy in less than a day. I'd never even had one girl before, and I didn't want to risk it with Sara, who smelled like cigarettes and alcohol and bad news.

"Maybe I should leave you and your friends alone. I have to find Blake."

I walked through the swinging doors and back into the kitchen.

"Duuuuude, you gotta hava beer," this guy by the kegs told me, offering a plastic cup.

"Nah, that's okay," I told him. "Drink it for me."

"Yeah? Thanks!"

I felt like the whole party was closing in around me. The music was giving me a headache and I couldn't think straight.

I stumbled over to a hallway and tried to quiet the pounding in my head. If the music would just go away for five minutes, I'd be fine. Maybe if I could sit down in one of the rooms?

I pushed down the handle on the closest door and walked inside. The room had this sickeningly sweet smell that reminded me of Blake.

There were a bunch of people in hooded sweatshirts sitting on the floor, smoking bowls, and surrounded by half-empty bags of junk food. I didn't see Blake.

"Anyone know a guy named Blake?" I asked.

One girl looked up at me and blinked slowly.

"Jake?"

"No, Blake. This is his party. Oh, never mind," I said, backing out into the hallway.

I clamped my hands over my ears and took a couple steps back toward the staircase, head held low, trying to avoid everything, but most of all the pounding music.

I climbed up another flight of stairs, looking for people who could answer my questions. It wasn't like I was going to find the Hilliard Chess League hidden on the third floor of a New York house party, but still.

A door was closed, and light flickered through the crack at the bottom. I could hear a TV playing.

"Hello?" I asked, knocking.

No one answered. I opened the door.

"Screw you, Sara! I don't know where your stupid Scotch glasses are!" Blake yelled, his eyes still glued to the screen.

"Blake?"

He turned around, and I noticed the huge circles under his eyes, the hint of a beard on his face, the tousled hair, the wrinkled T-shirt.

"Charley? What are you doing here?"

"Didn't you get the five voice mails I left you? I came to get trashed at your crazy party," I said sarcastically. "What do you think I'm doing here? I came to find you. We all did. Skylar and Marissa and me, I mean."

His eyes flickered back to the television set for a moment, and I looked too. A plastic bag swirled in the wind. He was watching *American Beauty* on a huge LCD screen.

Blake glared at me.

"I should have turned you in to Bloom for violating dorm visitation rules. You would have gotten it bad. Two women in the same night. A new Milbank record—Casanova Morton."

"What are you talking about?" I asked. "Blake, you're not making sense."

"You know what doesn't make sense?" he asked, eyes flashing. "What you're doing here. Do you think I'm going back to Hilliard with you?"

"Obviously."

"I'm not. I'm as good as expelled."

He turned the volume up on the television.

"So do something about it," I said angrily. "You're not expelled yet."

"What do you care, anyway?" Blake asked. "You've got your perfect life, perfect grades, perfect lay."

"Is that what you think of Skylar?" I asked.

He shrugged.

"That's really awful. Do you honestly think you deserve a girl like that if all she is to you is the perfect lay?"

"Like you deserve her more?" Blake shot back.

"Damn right I do. She took every prize I ever wanted, and, in the end, all I wanted was her. And not just to have sex with. To see what came of it. You don't know her anymore. And I don't know you."

He laughed hollowly.

"I'm the same as always."

"Bullshit. Blake, you are so screwed up right now. I don't even know what you're on. You weren't like this freshman year."

"I was fourteen!"

"Well, we're only seventeen! And besides, you can't justify what you're doing because you're older now. If anything, that only makes it worse. You know better than this, Blake. *You're* better than this."

"If I'm better than this, then why am I . . ."

He stopped and muted the television, but didn't say anything else.

"Why are you what?" I asked.

"Never mind," Blake said. "You wouldn't understand. Fuck. My parents are going to kill me."

"If it makes you feel any better," I said, sitting down on the edge of the bed, "my parents are going to kill me, too.

And not just because I ran away to New York. Because I called my dad today and told him that I wanted to study music at NYU."

"No shit," Blake said. "You're not going to study in Morton Library at Harvard?"

"It's called Widener Library," I said. "But no, I'm not."

"So you should be thanking me, then," Blake said, smirking. "If I hadn't taken off, you'd still be a miserable pre-pre-med."

It was then that the door opened and Marissa and Skylar walked in. Skylar, I was horrified to see, was dragging Sara behind her.

"Hey, Charlie'sh Angels!" Sara slurred, recognizing me.

Skylar caught my eye questioningly, but I just shrugged.

"Hi, Blake," Skylar said. "Start packing."

"Yeah, we found him," Marissa said into a cell phone. "Are you still downstairs? We'll meet you outside in five. Thanks, Kyle."

17

Skylar: When Helliard Freezes Over

It was so totally the same situation I'd been in during convocation: Blake was back, and my shoes were giving me blisters like you wouldn't believe. Okay, maybe not exactly the same situation. But still.

We dragged Blake out of the town house with his duffel bag half open. Sara had followed us out to the curb.

"Um, are you leaving with us?" I asked her sweetly.

She looked confused, and then her face went greenish.

"Oh God," she moaned, staggering back a couple steps and vomiting all over a trash can lid.

"Damn, Sara," Blake mumbled. "That's nasty."

I whirled on him, trying to keep my attention away from the tall twenty-one-year-old hovering at the edge of my peripheral vision.

"You think that's disgusting?" I asked. "That's what you were like after the party in Schwartz Theater."

I heard someone chuckling and knew it was Kyle.

"Takes 'he who smelt it, dealt it' to a new level, huh, Blake?" Kyle said, and I turned around to face him for the first time since I was fifteen.

He had put on maybe fifteen pounds. The extra bulk made him look older than twenty-one. Kyle had the door to one of those minivan cabs open and was leaning against the door frame.

"Hey," I said. "Thanks for getting the cab."

I ducked inside the cab and took one of the seats in the back. Everyone else climbed in, too, although Kyle pretty much pushed Blake inside.

"I am not taking the sick girl in my cab," the driver said.

I looked outside and saw some girls helping Sara back into the house.

"Don't worry," Marissa told him. "She's not coming."

I could feel Blake staring at me during the ride back to our hotel, but I just gazed out the window at the tops of the buildings and thought about how cold the city looked at night, how uninviting.

When we got up to the suite, Blake let out a low whistle.

"Well, you guys are certainly doing New York in style."

"My friend's parents keep this suite. It's borrowed," I told him.

Charley and I sat on the edge of the bed. Marissa and Kyle split the couch. Blake leaned against the glass of the balcony doors.

"Oh, that's just perfect," Blake muttered. "Skylar's already in bed with Charley. Slut."

Slut? *Slut?* Was he calling *me* a slut?

"No one in this room is a slut," I said. "Except maybe you."

"What-fucking-ever. You slept with my *brother* and lied about it!"

I could almost hear the studio audience whooping, "Jerry! Jerry!" in the background. Classy.

"Blake. Come on. I'm a virgin. Yes, I fooled around with your brother, and I'm sorry I didn't tell you. But I didn't have *sex* with him. My God, I was hardly fifteen. Who told you that?"

I stole an uncomfortable glance at Kyle. I hadn't seen him for two years, and now we were talking about it. About the reason we hadn't seen each other. About why it was over, and about why I still felt guilty.

"Doris Kim," Blake finally countered.

"Ooohhhhh," I mocked, wiggling my fingers in the air. "Doris Kim is such a reliable source of information. So trustworthy. Tell me again, whose boyfriend was she caught in a hot tub with last spring break?"

"Okay," he conceded. "Maybe you didn't sleep with him. But why didn't you tell me, huh?"

"Puh-leeze," Marissa broke in. "It was the last day of school and you were in the nurse's office with a migraine, remember?"

Blake flushed.

"Blake," Kyle broke in. "We talked about this last night. It wasn't Skylar's responsibility to tell you anything. We were both wrong. I should have been the one to tell you, because it was my fault for even going there."

"What were we supposed to do?" I added, "IM you about the whole debacle?"

"Maybe I believe you," Blake said. "But what about you and Charley?"

I sighed. "There was absolutely nothing going on between Charley and me before this. . . . It just happened today. I know you like me, and I think that's really cool, but I've only ever seen you as a friend. A good friend."

"Fine. Everything's goddamn perfect and we're all bestest buddies. Satisfied?" Blake shot back.

I shrugged.

"Not really," Charley said. "You ran away. Shit, Blake, McCabe came looking for you. I'm sick of covering for you. I get that you're not having the best time dealing with your parents, but you don't need to lie about it. We know. We just haven't rubbed it in your face. We get that you're going through a lot of stuff. Why else are we here?"

"I don't know. Why?" Blake challenged.

"To rescue you from your life of prostitution," Marissa piped up.

"I'm not selling myself on the streets," Blake scoffed.

"You are," Marissa insisted. "In your own way. You've sold yourself—your future—for a few drunken nights and bottles of pills." She got up and walked over to the window. "Was it worth it? Did whoever you got your stash from get their money's worth? They took what you could have been. God, Blake. You look awful. And when you ran away from school, look where you went—to stay with a girl, who's just as bad as you are. We thought we were coming here to find our friend, but maybe this was just a big mistake. You're not even grateful. We all saved your ass tonight, and we all risked our transcripts coming here, but you don't seem to care."

Marissa was standing next to Blake, so she was literally yelling into his face.

"Way to go," I told Blake.

Blake had this funny look on his face, like he couldn't believe what he'd heard, or where he was, or what he'd done.

Then, so softly I almost missed it, Blake said, "I'm sorry."

"What?" I asked, to be sure.

"I said I'm sorry," he muttered. "I didn't mean to wreck your applications or make you think I sold my soul for a couple lousy bottles of Klonopin."

"That's better," I said.

"Better," Kyle agreed, "but Blake still doesn't get it. He doesn't understand how many people care about him and he doesn't know what great friends he has. You guys actually came after him. That's amazing."

"You came after him, too," Charley pointed out.

"Of course I did. He's my kid brother," Kyle said.

"We're not going to have a chick flick moment now, are we?" Blake asked, rolling his eyes.

"No," Kyle said. "And I hope we'll never have to. Charley, Marissa, Skylar, I want you guys to keep an eye on Blake for me. If he does anything wrong at Hilliard, and I'm talking one toke or wine cooler, go straight to the counselor he'll be seeing twice a week from now on. Blake doesn't want to know what I'll do to him if he screws up again."

"It doesn't matter," Blake said. "They're not going to take

me back. I'm expelled the second I show up back on campus. The DC is probably waiting for me."

"What are you talking about?" Kyle said. "You think I didn't fix things? As soon as I reached Sara and confirmed that you'd showed up in the city, I called Hilliard and pretended to be Dad."

"You did?" Blake asked, perking up.

"Of course. I called the school first thing yesterday and told them we had a family emergency and I'd sent your brother to pick you up the night before, and hopefully he hadn't forgotten to sign you out for a few days."

"Thanks," Blake said. "I owe you, man."

"Well, you'll be repaying your debt by staying sober for the next nine months, and by getting help. No screwing around with the counselor, either." Kyle shook his head. "I know it's hard that Mom and Dad have been so preoccupied lately, but one of us is going to have to fill them in on what's been going on, and I'm hoping it will be you. Don't worry, I'll be there for you. I'm not going to stand back and watch you make a mess out of your life. And your friends won't, either."

"Fine. I get it, okay? When do we go back?" Blake asked.

"Now," Charley said. "I mean, as soon as we can. Skylar and Marissa and I are going to get hell for spending a night out of the dorms and missing a day and a half of classes. We should get back before we get nailed with more broken rules."

"I hate to break it to you," I said, "but it's not like we can just hop on the MetroNorth train at one in the morning."

"Shit," Charley said.

"What if we call Mr. McCabe?" Marissa suggested.

That actually wasn't a bad idea.

"Maybe he can cover for us," I added.

Charley shrugged. "Let's do it," he said.

I opened up my backpack, took out my school folder, and removed Mr. McCabe's class syllabus. Then I took out my phone and dialed the number.

"Yuhhhhh?" Mr. McCabe groaned.

"Mr. McCabe?" I asked.

"Yes. Who's this?"

"It's Skylar, from your creative writing class?"

"It's the middle of the night. Is everything okay?" Now he sounded wide awake.

"Everything's fine. I'm okay. Well, not just me. Charley and Marissa, too. And Blake."

"But I was told yesterday that Blake was signed out for a family emergency."

"Oh, about that . . . um, we can explain everything, but I'm going to need, like, the hugest favor ever."

"Should I get my car keys?" He sighed.

"You should probably get a tank of gas to go with it," I whispered guiltily. "We're in SoHo, at the SoHo Grand."

"I'll be there in two hours. You better climb into my car with an enormous cup of the strongest coffee known to mankind, because I'll need it."

"Check on the giant coffee front. And thanks for coming to get us."

"Don't mention it. I'm deducting a point off your final grade for every mile I have to drive."

"What?"

"Kidding. Although I'm serious about needing one hell of an explanation for this."

"I know. Okay, thanks. Bye."

I hung up.

"He says two hours," I reported.

"Where are you going to sleep tonight, Kyle?"

He shrugged. "Don't worry. Maybe I'll call up a friend at Columbia and see if I can crash in his dorm."

"It's late. You could stay here," I suggested. "It's free, and besides, I need someone to give the key to my friend Callie in the morning."

"That would be great," Kyle said appreciatively. "Thanks, Skylar. I didn't . . . I mean . . ."

"You're welcome," I said firmly. I didn't want to cancel out the present and start rechecking my past problems.

Kyle grabbed the remote control in response and flipped on the TV. He jumped channels for a minute and then stopped on a classic eighties movie that had just started.

Marissa staked her claim on the remaining couch. Charley climbed into the bed, and I shook my head slightly, because I didn't think Blake was ready to watch us snuggle. I dragged the desk chair closer to the television and curled up. I saw Blake sprawl out on the bottom of the bed, looking exhausted.

It was just like being back in Milbank, watching a movie. Except this time the bed was big and luxurious, and the room was a luxury suite, not a Milbank double. And it felt like the summer was already ending, or at least starting to wind down. Our last summer session together.

By the time Mr. McCabe called me back to say he was outside at the curb, it was almost three in the morning. I'd ordered a coffee from room service, and when we walked outside to meet him, I proffered the steaming cup.

"Is Starbucks even open this late?" McCabe asked.

"Nope, but room service is," I told him. "Thanks for coming to get us."

"I'm Kyle Dorsey," Kyle said, shaking Mr. McCabe's non-coffee-clutching hand. "Can I speak with you a moment, sir?"

The two of them walked a few yards away from us, so we couldn't hear what they were saying. But we all tried to listen in, anyway. I sampled their conversation, hearing small bits at a time.

". . . Really appreciate you taking them back to school."

". . . Family emergency?"

"Sorry about . . . but our father is . . . I'm sure you understand."

". . . take that into account. It was nice meeting you."

Kyle waved at us and headed back into the hotel. I wanted to say thank you for that, because I was sure he'd just covered for us with Mr. McCabe. I wanted to say so many things that I never could, and I knew he did too. But that was so long ago. Having Blake back had dredged up the past in a way I'd never thought possible.

We piled into Mr. McCabe's Land Rover, Blake in the front and the rest of us in the back. Our bags rattled around in the trunk as we drove through the deserted city streets.

New York was quiet in this muted way that I'd never really appreciated before. And it was still so warm outside that it didn't feel like nighttime at all, just like there was this timeless darkness.

It was comforting to know that I was going back to an old routine, an old structure. I finally felt like I was putting my reputation behind me. Charley liked me for who I was, and so did Marissa. She always had. Blake would forgive in time. What happened with his brother would haunt us less and less frequently until Kyle was just another guy I had gone to school with saying congrats at graduation.

Mr. McCabe put on a CD—to help him stay awake, he said—and Charley whispered to me that the band was called the Smiths.

"Do you have any tabs for this stuff?" Charley asked.

"Sure," Mr. McCabe said. "I'll give it to you after we've finished editing that guitar essay you turned in to me, so you can submit it with your college applications."

We waited for Mr. McCabe to say something else. To make some remark about our trip to New York City before we could talk together, figure out what it was Kyle told him, and get our story straight.

Mr. McCabe cleared his throat, and I momentarily panicked but then he smiled. I watched his eyes twinkle in the rearview mirror as he said, "You kids are crazier than Holden Caulfield."

"That I agree with," Charley said.

"Although I'll have you kids know that next time I tell my students to be the masters of their fate and captain their souls into uncharted waters, I'll specify that I don't mean crossing the Hudson."

We all laughed, relieved, and it was a great feeling. I smiled and rested my head against the window.

I must have fallen asleep, because the next thing I knew, we were driving through Hilliard's heavy wrought-iron gates. We were back. The four of us. The Hell Raisers. And I sort of had this feeling, as we climbed out of Mr. McCabe's Land Rover and walked through the heavy wooden doorway of Milbank Hall, that everything was going to turn out all right. Better than all right—better than yesterday.

18

Charley: To Be or Not to Be Valedictorian

In the end, Skylar and I wound up pretending the whole valedictorian thing didn't exist. We even convinced Headmaster Bell to call us the "top-ranked male and female students in the graduating class" and to let us combine our speeches at commencement.

The ceremony was held out on the grass in Hamilton Quad because the weather was decent and some pranksters had superglued a sofa to the middle of the gym floor (it was hell getting the glue off my fingers).

The whole ceremony was a mess of white folding chairs and a balloon arch in the Hilliard colors: green and navy blue.

I felt too warm in my blazer, uncomfortable in my stiff dress shoes. The girls all looked so innocent in white. I told Skylar that I liked her dress, which was tight in all the right places, only I didn't say that, and she smiled wryly and told me that this would be the last time most of these girls could get away with white dresses unironically.

When she said that, I realized how much I was going to miss everyone. We were graduating. We were leaving boarding school behind forever, going on to our separate colleges. It was unreal.

After that last summer, I'd been counting time from the Day I Realized I Wanted to Go to NYU and Hooked Up with Skylar. Seven weeks from then until the first day of school. Five months until college applications were due. Eight months until we all found out where we got in (we'd agreed to all find out on the same day, so none of us applied early decision). Ten months until the Graduation Gala, where Skylar and I got to wear these goofy-looking crowns and she didn't get too mad when I stepped on her shoes and got them kind of dirty. Ten months and one week until commencement.

I just didn't get how all that time had slipped by so quickly. But it had and there we were, a chessboard of dark blazers and white dresses, new class rings glinting on everyone's fingers.

Everyone was seated alphabetically in rows right in front of the stage, and on my back I could feel the seventy-five digital video cameras everyone's parents had pointed at us.

Headmaster Bell got up and welcomed everyone. I wondered if our graduation meant anything to him. He gave the same speech every year, wore the same hood and robes to the same ceremony year after year after year. The only thing that changed were the students. And I found the whole thing extremely depressing.

Everyone clapped, and Headmaster Bell took a seat at the

back of the stage. We all stood and sang the school song. It was as slow as a funeral dirge. At the end, the four of us yelled the line from *Rent,* "To being an us, for once, instead of a them!"

Headmaster Bell chuckled and shot us a look. I squirmed in my seat for a moment before I realized that he couldn't touch us. We were *graduating.*

Mr. Harcourt, the guidance counselor, walked up to the lectern. I remembered sitting in his office that past fall, telling him my top choice colleges. He'd looked over the tops of his glasses at me and asked if I was sure. I'd nodded, satisfied with my choices. Mine. Not my parents'.

Harcourt cleared his throat and rambled about how exceptional our class was that year, with six students headed off to Harvard, seven to Yale, and four to Princeton. We had at least one student going off to every Ivy League school in the country. Ours was the best class yet.

And I thought, *He'll say that again next year.*

Skylar and I were up next. Harcourt introduced us.

"Next you'll hear from the top-ranked boy and girl students in the graduating class, Charles Morton III and Skylar Banks. Charles is going to NYU next year, while Skylar is headed to MIT. They've deviated from the traditional speech form and have prepared a debate. Skylar, Charley?"

Everyone clapped. I could hear the whispers. *Who's valedictorian? Why didn't they say? And what's up with the debate?*

I took the lectern that was stage right. Skylar was stage left. I reached into my pocket for my note cards. She didn't have any, but I'd known that she wouldn't.

"The topic of our debate," Skylar said, "is whether we can attribute our readiness to step out into the world to the excellence of a Hilliard education, or to the friendships we forged while living on campus over the past four years. I will be speaking for friendship. Charley will be speaking for education. It's his opening."

I took a deep breath, looked down at my note cards, and began.

"When I was fourteen, I thought my parents knew everything. More than that, I thought they knew everything that was best for me. And they wanted me to be a doctor. But after three years at Hilliard, after AP bio and calc and Latin, I realized that I had a different career in mind: music. It is because of the wide array of courses offered here at Hilliard that I could discover my true interests in time to apply to the right college for me. If my teachers hadn't exposed me to the humanities and encouraged me to try out for the school paper and the school plays, I would never have had the confidence to decide my own future, and to pursue a liberal arts education."

I looked at Skylar.

"I learned a long time ago that two x plus three y is never five xy. We cannot combine unlike terms without breaking the rules of mathematics. But sometimes, when we are not looking for a solution, but rather a different way of viewing the problem, it is permissible, even appropriate, to break the rules. I have such a wonderful and diverse group of friends here, and Hilliard's social scene has allowed me to decide for myself who I will 'combine' with, and on what terms. It is in the dorms and through activities that we all choose who we will listen to, and what we will become. Sometimes our variable does not have to be represented by the letter A. Living with other teens, sharing experiences and relationships with them, is what makes Hilliard into the turning point between the candor of childhood and the limitless possibilities of adulthood. I only wish that the timeline of my life at Hilliard could have no endpoints, like the memories I will take away with me."

Damn. I was in serious danger. I shuffled my note cards and delivered my first point. When I was done and Skylar began talking, I took a good look at the graduating class.

Ever since April first, our names had been connected with schools. I was Charley NYU. To my side was Skylar MIT. And in front of me were Sticks Dartmouth, Hunter Harvard, Janice Cornell, Marissa Mount Holyoke, Blake Kings, Alison Penn, Catcher Stanford, Eunice Tufts, Doris Columbia, Shirley Brown, and a hundred others.

We were a handful of confetti, waiting to be scattered and blown all over the place.

Especially the four of us. Marissa was going to be less than two hours away from Skylar in Massachusetts, but Blake was going all the way to Kings College in London, and who knew when we'd see him again. There was a three-hour train ride between Skylar and me, and I couldn't wait to meet her on the platform and ride the subway holding her close again, like last summer.

I didn't want it to be over. I didn't want to be one of those old WASPs in a seersucker jacket and deck shoes, reminiscing about his boarding-school days, trying to get his kid to understand the best years of his life, but forgetting to understand his kid.

I shifted my gaze. I could see Blake's parents sitting next to mine, my mom leaning out into the aisle with a camera, my kid brother with a handheld game, some sort of portable PlayStation. My dad.

He was wearing his school tie, that decrepit thing I'd tried to throw out when I was ten, tried to hide when I was twelve, and tried to pretend I hadn't hid when I was thirteen and he found the thing behind some books in his study. And I sort of liked him for wearing it here, because I got that it meant he was proud of me and wanted people to know I had followed in his footsteps, even though I wasn't going to be a doctor, even though I wasn't the clear winner for valedictorian, even though I'd given my brother all my old Harvard stuff for Christmas.

In the end, Skylar won the debate. It really was about friendship, not class rank or getting nominated for an "Exemplary Student Spotlight" in the yearbook. And I'd known it all along. I'd just let her say it, because even though I'd known it, she'd believed it.

The diploma, when I got it, was so small in my hand. A black leather flipbook, embossed, the size of a DVD case. I knew my dad would hang it up in his study, making a little row of Hilliard diplomas: Charles Morton, Charles Morton Jr., and Charles Morton III.

After the ceremony, a photographer motioned for the whole class to get together on the stage, and a couple of guys were laughing and pretending to use the tissue paper inside their diploma cases as rolling papers, which made Mr. Harcourt give an impromptu lecture on decorous behavior, as if it wasn't too late.

Blake, who I was standing near, muttered, "Goddamn potheads."

I grinned. After the trip to New York, Blake's idea of an herbal refreshment was an iced tea. Little by little, he was getting back to the way he used to be when we were freshmen. It must be hard, especially since he also had to deal with Skylar and me dating, but he was doing it. And in my opinion, that was worth more than any Ivy League diploma.

Marissa, who was also standing near us, had a small stuffed owl with a rolled-up diploma in its beak that she wanted to hold in the photo. She'd curled her hair for graduation, and it made her look older somehow.

Skylar put her hand on my back as the photographer lined up the shot. I felt my spine sharpen and tingle with expectation as the photographer counted down, three, two, one, and I turned toward Skylar and kissed her.

That portrait would hang on the wall over the stairs. No matter how far apart the four of us were, we would always be in Milbank Hall.

Acknowledgments

• • • • • • • • • • • •

This book would not exist without my incredible agent, Susan Schulman, whose e-mails I loved so much that I felt the need to publish them on the Internet; my amazing editor, Jodi Keller, whose fashion sense and editorial genius have yet to be surpassed by any other savvy New Yorker; and my wonderful publisher, Beverly Horowitz.

Then there are the friends to whom I totally owe everything. Infinite thank-yous to: my best friend, blog buddy, nightly telephone call confidante, and fellow YA author Lauren Barnholdt; my e-mail mentor Caren Lissner; Marty Beckerman for endlessly hilarious AIM conversations about writing; Professor William Sharpe at Barnard College for "Invictus"; Maggie Chan for the CUnity prank; the Linker family for letting me finish my edits at their kitchen table on New Year's Eve; the Pure Fiction League critique group, for PLS and a very great time every Thursday night; the St. Michael's Academy debate team for stories (especially Chris Hillyard for letting me borrow his excellent last name, which I misspelled); the Philolexian Society at Columbia University for wit, debate, and podilectern pride; my aunts and uncles; everyone on my LiveJournal friends list; the Other Robyn; Melodye Shore; Devorah Rose; Sheila; Jade; Polina for running away to New York City with me every weekend; and Skylar from P.E. at Northwood (whose name I borrowed).

Now for the inanimate, plural, and just plain silly thanks: my eighth-grade crush (whose blog provided the inspiration for Blake), all of my students at Etum Academy summer session, and the WB show *Young Americans* (which never should have been canceled).